It's always fine weather when good friends get together

The whole of London swam in a great, green fog, a proper pea souper, the sort of fog the old town had not known for years and years and thought itself done with forever.

"We three," said the man in black, "would make quite an army."

"Separately, we have achieved much," murmured the old man at the rack. "There is no imaginable limitation to what we could accomplish together!"

"The glorious slaughters," rumbled the man in the mask. "The refinements and extensions of torture. *Mon Dieu*, the screams!"

"The treasures we might garner in!" the old man said looking up, a new light in his rheumy eyes, "all that lovely money to count and stack!"

The tall man smiled down at them with his green cat's-eyes. "And the power, gentlemen," he said. "The ability to crush!"

There was a longer, even more thoughtful silence, and then the man in black extended a large, gloved hand.

"The possibilities are altogether too delightful to

EVERYBODY'S FAVORITE DUCK

GAHAN WILSON

THE MYSTERIOUS PRESS

New York • London
Tokyo • Sweden • Milan

Mysterious Press books are published in association with
Warner Books, Inc.
666 Fifth Avenue
New York, N.Y. 10103

W A Warner Communications Company

Printed in the United States of America

Originally published in hardcover by The Mysterious Press.
First Mysterious Press Paperback Printing: December, 1989

10 9 8 7 6 5 4 3 2 1

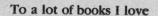

To a lot of books I love

Prologue

The whole of London swam in a great, green fog, a proper pea souper, the sort of fog the old town had not known for years and years and thought itself done with forever.

Children wondered at it, astounded, and tested the bitter, oily taste of it with their tongues; sentimental older folk's eyes watered, not just from chemical irritation, but from wistful nostalgia brought on by memories of bygone fogs of their youth which had been this thick and this vile, and by recollections of the wonderful and awful things which had happened in those romantic, long gone, murky swirlings.

Older British books dealing with mysterious themes often lovingly describe such fogs and thereby innocently mislead contemporary readers of romantic inclination, especially Americans and Japanese, until their hopes are dashed by hotel porters or taxi drivers regretfully assuring them that nowadays, sir or madam, such fogs never happen.

But now it *was* happening, and moment by moment growing more spectacularly thick and opaque, and though it might be delighting tourists and children and old folk, it was causing considerable confusion and dismay in official circles.

Government vehicles were everywhere, detecting

and recording various aspects of the phenomenon: Droplets were being blotted up to see which colors they would turn to when treated with reagents, other droplets were being teased into test tubes for later evaluation, and many pins were being stuck into many maps.

It would only be far later, after a wide variety of computers stuffed with data on the fog had been brought on-line and shared their contents, that baffled officials would have their chance to puzzle long and fruitlessly over the numerous, simultaneous fires, private and industrial, which produced the smoke which had then conspired with the very odd, not to say strange, atmospheric conditions only just that moment prevailing, to create the fog.

Nor did it do much more than confuse officialdom further when another computer told it a little later on that the fires were mostly of suspicious origin; nor was it of any aid to learn there had been a mysterious, sleek aircraft of an entirely unknown design flying over London minutes before the fog developed, since no computer or bureaucrat ever learned that that aircraft had been there for the sole pupose of seeding the upper atmosphere with sparkling ice crystals containing strange chemicals in order that the glorious fog might begin.

And of course no one in officialdom ever so much as dreamed that the whole thing had been done just for old time's sake.

A burly chauffeur in an ominous dark uniform with shiny iron buttons and disquieting insignia subliminally suggestive of various sinister military organizations of the past marched smartly to the rear half of a long Rolls Royce, which gleamed with a ghostly, fishy luster under a thin coating of the fog's droplets. Very respectfully, the chauffeur opened the car's rear door; very warily he moved back so as to be out of the occupant's way.

An extremely tall, extremely thin man in an Astrakhan hat and a long cape with a high fur collar unfolded himself in a smooth, serpentine undulation, stepped out of the car, and sniffed the fog with the loving appreciation of a true connoisseur. His desiccated face was Oriental, shriveled as an Egyptian mummy's, and owned a queer calmness which suggested a Buddha—but a suspect, devious Buddha, one altogether lacking in compassion, a Buddha whose followers would undergo strange and occasionally fatal enlightenments.

The fog he'd sampled exited soundlessly in two thin, smoky lines from his nostrils, a dragon's exhalation, and as he gave a satisfied cat's blink, his eyes somehow managed to pick up a stray shaft of light even in this dank gloom and shoot a yellow-green gleam back into the surrounding darkness.

He stepped across the sidewalk so that he stood before the entrance of a sooty Victorian building whose wet, dirty bricks glistened like pudlets of dried blood which the fog had once again made moist. Mounted across the front of the building, just above the first story, a series of large, elaborate wooden letters caked in peeling gilt combined to read: MADAME GRIMMAUD'S WAX MUSEUM.

The tall man reached out a long, bony finger and pressed a button set into the wall by the side of the entrance. Almost immediately the door was opened by a tiny but dangerous-looking man in a black burnoose who cringed at the sight of the visitor and backed away from his path, retreating with the careful, high steps of a spider since his rearward path took him over the swollen bulk of a large dead man sprawled belly-up on the floor and dressed in a guard's uniform with "Grimmaud's Museum" sewn in gold on its cap and over the corpse's heart.

With no hesitation, walking with the confidence of

one in a familiar place, the tall man crossed the large main room of the establishment. He entirely ignored the many wax effigies of the powerful and celebrated displayed in splendor on roped-off platforms and kept his full attention fixed on an ominous, stone-rimmed entrance at the rear of the hall.

Mounted above the door of that entrance was a solemnly gaudy Gothic sign in bold black letters, lit as mysteriously as possible by a purposely flickering lamp. The sign read first: *L'OUBLIETTE*, and then, beneath, *THE DUNGEON OF HORROR*. The outer corners of his nearly lipless mouth lifted briefly in a kind of smile as he passed through the entrance and padded his way down a winding flight of steps.

Doughty British laborers of bygone years had labored long and hard to make those steps look as though they might descend to the deepest bowels of an ancient Bavarian castle, but, in fact, they spiraled down to a singularly bizarre basement which was the very commercial heart of the Grimmaud establishment.

To be sure, the wax museum prided itself on its excellent likenesses of the respectable folk upstairs, and did its very best to have effigies of all the latest politicians, actors and, of course, every single member of the royal family on hand, but the denizens of this dark, stuffy, depressing room were what really pulled the tourists, international and domestic. Ever since old Madame Grimmaud herself had escaped the French Revolution and started the business with sullen, gory figures sculpted by her own thin hands, this basement, or others like it, had given the place its real reputation.

Here, in this gloomy, dusty place, which now and then shook faintly as the train in the Underground roared by beneath it, lurked grim wax statues of notorious murderers of the past and present, sometimes with the very things they had used to murder and mutilate, the same knives and roped chairs and nicked hatchets. Here, too, were on display the grisly devices which so many of these rascals had eventually encountered: the nooses which had strangled them, the guillotines which had chopped off their wincing heads, and the iron chairs they'd been chained in as they roasted.

The tall man paused at the foot of the stairs and studied the back of a gaunt, elderly party who had arrived before him and was interestedly prodding a wax dummy tied in frozen agony upon a supposedly authentic rack of the Inquisition.

Aside from a cobwebby fringe hanging dismally from its rear, the huge, bulging head of the old man toying with the tortured dummy was entirely bald, and its unwholesome skin suggested the pallid flesh of a squid grown pale from hiding too long in clouds of its own ink. When the old man slowly turned, guided by that sure and certain instinct given to creatures talented in sneaking, the face of that ominous head was shown to be just as pale, save for the remarkably dark pits around its sunken eyes. The old man studied the new arrival from beneath the enormous bulge of his pale, bald forehead in a studiously cold, scientific manner.

"You are late," he said, after a longish pause, regarding the tall man with a peculiar waving motion of his head.

"No," said the other, in a harsh, sibilant whisper, "you are early. I have never met you yet but that I have not found you lurking in wait."

"Of course there's no sign of the Frenchman," said the other irritatedly, turning back to the rack and giving its handle a little tug, which made the dummy creak. "But then the people of that nation have no appreciation of the value of time whatsoever."

"I have been here all along, English," said a deep voice from a dark corner, and the two others turned at a stirring of old chains in one of the dark, dusty corners of the room just in time to see the graceful appearance of a large man dressed in impeccable evening attire.

There was no visible flesh about him, save for his burning eyes, for his high-domed head was entirely and neatly covered by a tailored black-silk mask which disappeared under the immaculately white wings of his shirt collar with a tidy ascot fold, and his large, long-fingered hands were hidden under faintly gleaming gloves, also of black silk. As they watched he sauntered further into visibility, letting them see he'd acquired a horrendous antique mace from one of the exhibitions.

"I could have killed you any number of times, Professor. With this, for instance," he said, twirling the mace idly and easily in spite of the fact it must have weighed at least fifty pounds. "I could have splattered your celebrated brains on the floor of this filthy place. Your mangled body would have made an excellent exhibit."

"For your sake, it is just as well you didn't try," said the old man at the rack, showing his yellowed teeth in a very nasty smile, "as I have made certain arrangements—which, no offense, gentlemen, I see no point in revealing to either one of you prematurely—to ensure that any such ill-advised move would be both unsuccessful and fatal to yourselves."

From the toss of his head it seemed the man in the mask had found no difficulty in framing an appropriate reply, but the tall man with the cape stilled both his companions with a regal sweep of his hand.

"No bickering, gentlemen!" he spat. "You forget our purpose. Or is this convocation feckless? Have we gathered here to change the world, or are we merely met in combat? Do you join me, or do you die?"

The two men glared fiercely up at him with a combined menace of appalling force which would have caused most recipients to fall on their knees and beg for mercy, but the tall man only studied the others thoughtfully for a moment, then made a tiny bow and spread his long-taloned hands palms-forward in a gesture of truce.

"Excuse me, I have the habit of command. Perhaps I spoke too forcefully," he said, lowering his voice, with some difficulty, down to a guttural whisper. "We are— all three of us—too used to having our own way. I do not wish to demean your talents or denigrate your dangerousness. If I did not think of you as my equals I would not have suggested this meeting in the first place."

The two others relaxed, just a little, as the other continued.

"I chose this room for our historic meeting as it most singularly evokes the past, very much including our own, and is full of lessons for us all." He paused and tapped his fingertips together. "By the way, speaking of things nostalgic, did you enjoy the fog I had put on? I thought it might induce in us an appropriately ruminative mood."

After a moment of silence, the man at the rack gave its handle another tweak which wrenched the dummy into an even more frightful contortion.

"I did," he said. "I confess I did. Quite thoughtful of you to arrange it. Standing in it, just outside the museum, I was taken back to the time my organization succeeded in removing the crown jewels from the Tower of London. We had them all, you know, down to the last scepter and globe! For two whole weeks. Of course the public never knew of it. I hadn't thought of that in years. We committed real crimes back then, the sort of stuff these tacky swindlers operating nowadays daren't dream of!"

He sighed and reached down to fondle a curl or two of the dummy. Meanwhile the man in the mask had rested his mace at the base of the guillotine and was gazing thoughtfully up at the rusty streaks on its slanting blade.

"Oh, but you could kill gorgeously when there were fogs like that," he murmured. *"Bon gré mal gré*, and no one the wiser. One could improvise delightfully. Yes, I liked it very much. *Merci beaucoup.* And you were wise to have chosen this hall of murder and pain as our meeting ground, Mandarin. There is much here that touches us all."

He strode over to another side of the room, circled his huge, black-gloved hand around the neck of a bearded dummy, and plucked it from its stand.

"We called this one 'The Gnawer,' after the gargoyle on Notre Dame, because he was terrible with those he killed," he said, gazing at the dummy's eyes as Hamlet had gazed at Yorick's skull. "He was hanged because they caught him chewing through the neck of a little whore when he should have been following my orders and watching a certain box at the Opera. He cost me a lot of money, this one; he ruined a highly satisfactory plan."

He hurled the dummy brutally to the floor so that its wax head shattered and the pieces skittered in all directions like panicked crabs.

"It's true, what you say about this place," said the man at the rack. "How we're all of us involved in these displays. Take that group of dummies over there representing a heap of charred cadavers, the ones who were come upon one morning in what was left of the House of Lords. They got that way botching the installation of an explosive apparatus of my own invention which, had it been properly placed and activated and operated, would have forced the government to hand me over a fortune. I must say it does give me some small satisfaction to see their agonizing deaths so graphically depicted."

The tall man on the stairway nodded.

"Like yourselves, gentlemen," he hissed softly, "a quantity of my past endeavors are represented here by former associates and enemies rendered in wax with varying degrees of mediocrity. I even see a few infernal devices of my making, or simulations of them. But they are not cause for pride, no cause at all, because, of course, they represent failures, gentlemen, *failures!*"

He strode down into the room and stalked from dummy to dummy, striking one on the shoulder so the dust rose in a puff from its coat, knocking another's rat-chewed moustache askew on its lip with a hard slap, giving a third a contemptuous shove in the back which caused it to topple and split open on its own ax.

"These murderers and thieves are here because they were all caught, gentlemen, their crimes all went awry, and not a few of their blunders endangered ourselves!" He paused, standing by the fallen image of a more than ordinarily notorious strangler and crushed its mad stare into its grimy, pale face with slow, sure pressure from his slippered foot, then continued in a calmer tone. "Speaking for myself, it is only a matter of luck our own likenesses are not displayed here for the ignorant to gape at."

The stooped man at the rack nodded grimly.

"I must confess I have had the selfsame thought on previous visits to this establishment," he muttered softly.

The masked man broke off the head of a hunchbacked figure with a loud, startling pop.

"This one almost did such a thing to me," he snarled.

The tall man started slightly at this and raised one of his bony talons thoughtfully.

"Most interesting you point out that particular villain, as he bears most particularly on an important aspect of what we are here to discuss," he said. "That person's failure to kill a courier passing through the *Gare de Lyon* nearly led to your arrest, is that not so?"

The eyes of the burly man in black bore through the holes in his mask with increased intensity.

"That is true," he said.

"He did not kill that courier because I had paid him a higher price to kill another one here in London," the tall man said; then, as the man in black was somehow suddenly standing next to him with his gloved hands nearly at the tall man's throat: "Please understand I intended you no harm. Only later, when the failure of your plan to steal the train containing the gold was announced in the press, did I realize I'd placed you in mortal danger."

After a significant pause, the man in black lowered his hands.

"I have done the same for you," he said, and shrugged. "The *Invalides* business, for instance. That little trap under the dome was set for the *agents de police*, not for yourself. On my word, I had no idea you were even interested in the place at that time."

"I believe you," said the tall man, and then, turning to the ancient at the rack: "As you must believe me, Professor, when I assure you—"

"That the poisonous spiders I encountered when unrolling that papyrus were not intended for myself but for the greedy Dr. Benson," the other finished for him. "Of course I recognized your touch and have held the incident against you ever since. Very well, but then you must accept that the mine in the Thames which annihilated your motor launch was pure accident." When he saw the tall man nod he continued: "I take your point. We have inadvertently caused one another a great deal of bother down through the years. It would simplify matters considerably if we could manage to avoid stepping on the others' toes."

"We can avoid that easily and simply by merely stepping together, gentlemen," the tall man said. "I propose we do just that. I propose we *march!*"

There was a thoughtful silence.

"We three," said the man in black, "would make quite an army."

"Separately, we have achieved much," murmured the old man at the rack, ruminatively running a knobby finger along the twisted lips of the dummy. "There is no imaginable limitation to what we could accomplish together!"

"The glorious slaughters," rumbled the man in the mask. "The refinements and extensions of torture. *Mon Dieu*, the screams!"

"The treasures we might garner in!" the old man said looking up, a new light in his rheumy eyes, "all that lovely money to count and stack!"

The tall man smiled down at them with his green cat's-eyes.

"And the power, gentlemen," he said. "The ability to crush!"

There was a longer, even more thoughtful silence, and then the man in black extended a large, gloved hand.

"The possibilities are altogether too delightful to resist," he said, simply.

"I should never forgive myself for not undertaking the experiment," said the old man, raising a pallid claw.

"We are joined, then," concluded the tall man triumphantly and clutched the others' hands with a strong, spidery grip over the figure on the rack.

Did it stir when those three made contact? Of course not, since it was, after all, only a sooty, rather pathetic little statue. For all its writhing and grimacing it could not possibly move of itself no matter what awful things took place around it. For the same reason it also had to be an illusion that there was the faintest sound of a dusty rustling in the surrounding gloom, as if a shudder had run through the assembled wax murderers when those hands touched and those evil fingers webbed together. Crippen did not cringe and clutch his little bottle of poison tighter, for instance, and Jack the Ripper did not totter and cling to his whore of the moment for support, and Haigh, the acid-bath murderer, certainly did not blanch.

Nevertheless, the very next day, just a little before teatime, a child dragged to Madame Grimmaud's Dungeon of Horror by his nanny—a child who should of course never have been taken to such a dreadful place except that his guardian could not defer a moment longer seeing the brand-new effigy, just put on display, that of little Henry Briggs, who had, after years of ignored complaints, finally killed his wife and made her into meat pies which he had put in the freezer and later eaten, one by one—that child (who, to tell the truth, was thoroughly enjoying his visit) reached out a tiny hand to pluck at his nanny's dress, and with the other, he pointed to a dummy representing the fiendish strangler Christie and asked her: "Why is that man so frightened, Miss Tootle?"

Miss Tootle gave a small, dry sniff, smiled coldly, and said: "Frightened? That lot? Not likely, dear."

But then she leaned a little closer and noticed the bulge of Christie's eyes.

"Well," she said, uncertainly, for once, "perhaps . . ." and then her voice drifted off in a manner which was highly satisfactory to the little boy as it began to dawn on her that there did seem to be something new and strange about the old familiar figure, after all.

"Why is he afraid, then, Miss Tootle?" the little boy asked again, but of course she did not answer directly, it was not her way; she only bustled herself and her charge up the sinister steps and out of the establishment with a speed unusual for one who ordinarily moved only with a stately tread, and that's how the little boy came to believe Christie really did look frightened, and so did the dark hangman by the stairs, and so did the head of Louis the Fourteenth sitting on a bloody stump in its niche in the wall. They were, he was sure of it now, every one of them afraid.

And the best part was that Miss Tootle was so rattled by it all that she let him bully her into an extra ice cream before she managed to pull herself together.

1

It was early on a hot summer Tuesday morning, six thirty-three if you want to get picky, when I saw a black stretch limo moving like an ocean liner along Maple Street in Elmsville, and I just barely managed not to stop my gaze from rising smoothly above the sparkly water pouring out of the tap, and gliding by a robin singing out on the lawn, and coming to a graceful rest on a can of coffee sitting on a shelf just to the right of the window.

The driver was pretty good but not quite good enough because I caught him slowing down right in front of the house, right where you had a square-on view of it and of me standing by the kitchen sink.

Maybe he had an excuse, maybe someone had tapped him unexpectedly on the shoulder behind those smoky, one-way windows, perhaps because that someone was having trouble getting a lens focused, but I caught the driver slowing down, and that way I knew to keep my gaze moving right along to the can of coffee with my hand following after, and I knew I'd done it well enough so that nobody in that limo had seen me see them, or managed to get anything on tape to show somebody else I'd seen them, no matter how close up they'd zoomed in on me or how many frames they had to play with, because I'm good, because I'm a lot better than that driver.

Nevertheless, I have to confess I was pretty mad because this meant somebody had figured out that Mr. Bowen of 257 Maple Street wasn't just this old guy up the block, they'd figured out he was me, and one way or another that had to put a big hitch in my retirement and I resented it because it's not easy to retire in my line of work, it's plenty hard to get old enough to do it, and I'd gone to a lot of trouble and I thought I'd pulled it off, but now it looked like I hadn't, after all.

The best thing I'd liked about retirement, and I realize I'm talking about it in the past tense these days, was that nobody wanted to kill me. For most of my life people had wanted to kill me, and some of them had made some pretty good tries at it, but here in Elmsville it was unlikely the idea had ever crossed any of my neighbors' minds since I was just Mr. Bowen, and nobody wanted to kill Mr. Bowen or even took him particularly seriously.

I'd worked hard at that and done my usual good job, and my guess is that if you'd asked any of those neighbors how long I'd been living here among them the bulk of them might overestimate by as much as five years, maybe longer. I was a fixture: Little kids around here had me as one of their first memories, old ladies expected me to help them with their shopping bags when they got tired or confused, and girl scouts knew I'd buy their cookies.

Anyhow, that was all over now, probably, so I began to make plans and little preparations for the coming day. I got a couple of holsters and guns out of their hiding place under the little trapdoor I'd put in by the bed where they'd been for a long, long time, and strapped them on in sneaky places and put a larger, deadlier weapon under some rags in a bucket alongside of a clipper and a hand rake and a trowel, and then I slipped on the scruffy old outfit I liked to wear doing messier chores because my plan was to trim the bushes and weed the lawn and otherwise keep moving around outside the house.

It turned out to be a pretty good plan because it put me just around the corner of the front porch next to a little pile of crabgrass when the neat man with the briefcase showed up, and that gave me the chance to lean into view from nowhere and nail him where he stood with a neighborly smile halfway between the sidewalk and the front steps.

He smiled back, of course, I'd have been pretty insulted if they'd sent along somebody who wasn't good enough to smile back, and asked me my retirement name.

"Mr. Bowen?"

I stood up slow and easy and friendly enough, and gave him an amiable Mr. Bowen nod as I put my right hand under the rags in the bucket I was holding in my left hand so it could get a good, firm grip on what I'd hidden there.

The man was a shade over thirty, probably got his sport jacket at a place that sells them for a little less than regular stores, had neat, close-cropped hair and a face like a young, sincere bulldog, and looked as if he could move pretty quickly and efficiently if it was called for. He really didn't like seeing my hand stay in that bucket, but since he was completely exposed on a tidy walkway in the middle of a sunny, well-mowed Elmsville lawn, there wasn't too much he could do about it.

"I'm Fred Perkins," he said, lifting his chin a little. "From the Beautiful Home Shop in the mall?"

He raised his briefcase, slowly, and opened it, slowly, keeping his bright little brown eyes on my big, bright blue ones, except for quick, guarded flickers at that bucket, and I was interested in him, too, and neither of our smiles faltered for a minute.

"Right," I said. "Mr. Perkins. Sure enough."

"I think I've got something that might interest you, sir," he said, and carefully lifted out a swatch of carpet and held it up so that anybody passing by or looking out of a neighboring window could see the roses on it clearly.

"Looks just like what I've been trying to find," I said, speaking in a friendly tone of voice just a trifle louder than I ordinarily would, and then I went on, still friendly, but a lot quieter. "You're holding that thing up like a flag. Let's go inside and see how it looks in a darkened hallway. You first. The door's unlocked because we don't lock doors much here in Elmsville because we don't get many visitors like you. And you're right, I do have something nasty in this bucket."

I watched him, not all that enthusiastically, as he went up the steps just ahead of me. Someone in his past had done too good a job of teaching him to walk like a soldier, for example, and the after-shave he used was sold with particularly dumb ads on tv.

I arranged to be right behind him through the door and I closed it with my foot and let the bucket drop the moment we got through so he could have a clear view of what I was pointing at the base of his throat, just above his collar. I always like to aim at visible flesh since you never know what kind of a trick outfit might be covering the rest of a person.

"I know this could be described as excessive firepower," I said, "almost in bad taste, but I always say you can't play it too safe with someone trying to sell you a carpet."

Going over him carefully with my other hand I found the police special I'd more or less expected, a nasty little Italian pistol which came as something of a surprise, and some ID—which he obviously hated to see me paw over—indicating he was a member in good standing of a governmental investigative agency I'd variously worked with and against through the years.

"I hope you realize you probably wouldn't have been able to get your hands on those so easily if my instructions weren't to let you see them in the first place," he said.

I gave him an ambiguous smile and a little push in order to move him along into the kitchen.

"Let's assume for the moment you're one of the good guys," I said. "I sincerely hope you are and that these cards of yours aren't lying, since, so long as I've been tracked down, that would be better than a number of other alternatives that could cross my mind. I assume you want me to call you George Ashman, like it says? How did you find me? Sit over there, keeping your hands on the table, and I'll pour us some coffee."

"I'll have mine light with no sugar," he said. "George Ashman is my name, and I am with the agency. I have other papers, other proofs, in my briefcase, along with a number of things we'd like you to see. I wouldn't want you to think it wasn't tough locating you. For a long time we couldn't get past Egypt, and we almost gave up on you in Paris."

"You weren't supposed to get past Egypt," I said. "I thought I'd died pretty well in Egypt."

"You did," he said. "You did the whole thing well and ordinarily we'd never have managed to find you, but finding you was given top priority, from the House. Not just to our outfit, but to every group we've got. The entire government of the United States of America was after you, sir."

I sat across from him after putting the coffee on the table, one cup at a time. I never let my weapon leave my hand, nor did I let it point anywhere but at his head. Taking things out item by item, according to my instructions, Ashman gave me a stack of very snappy documentation as to his being who and what he said he was, and then handed me a number of convincing-looking letters from important people I'd worked with before.

"Seems all these folks want me to hear you out, George," I said. "So let's spend a quarter hour at it and see what happens."

"Good," he said. "Can I call you by your right name? Can I call you John Weston?"

"I sort of hoped I'd never hear that name again, but so long as you're at it let's say you make it John, same as I've made it George, and then we can play at being friends and see if it takes."

He reached into his briefcase again, continuing to move slowly because I was still holding on to my weapon in spite of us being friends, took out a photograph, and pushed it across the table so it would come to me right-side up.

It wasn't a pretty photograph at all since it showed a lot of dead bodies and spatters of blood and things like that. The camera was looking into a room, a handsome room, oddly familiar; looking from the height of a tall man's face down at the floor where the bodies were, or most of them. There was one lying across a big desk by the windows and another draped over the arms of a large chair in back of the desk. Counting those two bodies and those on the floor you came out to nine.

The shooting must have interrupted a fairly formal occasion since all the dead people were decked out in neat, dark suits, and a number of them, especially the little cluster around the desk, looked to be pretty expensively tailored; there's no tougher test for a good suit than to have somebody shoot it full of holes and then have somebody else soak it with their blood and still have it drape nicely even if the person wearing it is sprawled in a crazy attitude on top of a fan of documents spread over a carpet and giving you a wide, meaningless grin with one eye staring at you and the other one shut.

After I'd taken the first photograph in, Ashman pushed another across the table at me and then some others and pretty soon I had quite a collection of them, each one considerately taken from a slightly different angle of the room so I wouldn't miss a thing, and all the time the room was growing more and more familiar. I knew for sure now I'd seen it a number of times, or other pictures of it, and I knew they weren't bloody ones like these.

Other items seemed familiar, too. There was one man, for instance, a plump fellow, with a distinct shape to his head, which was bald except for a neat strip of gray hair running from ear to ear, who I almost kept recognizing except for his face having been blown away. Again, like the room, I may never have actually seen him in person, but I knew that particular bald dome because he was somebody famous, somebody really famous.

It was another man, though, that really bothered me. He was bunched up against the side of the desk— something about his posture put me in mind of a kid hiding—and I knew him, I knew him personally. Something about his hands and shoulders made me sure of it. I knew his thick, strong fingers, but the camera was always shooting him so that he was looking the other way, sometimes only just, but always the other way.

"It's quite a slaughter," I said. "And they used some really serious weapons. Look at the wall here; I assume it was fancy plasterwork like the rest, but it's pulverized, it's rubble. And the whole corner of the desk looks like its been bashed off by a passing truck. I take it you want my expert opinion on all of this."

Then he handed me another photograph, and in this one the man bunched up by the desk, the one I knew I knew, was looking straight at the lens, straight at me. He looked pissed off, I supposed he'd look pissed off forever unless a mortician did something about it, and he had a gun halfway out of his shoulder holster.

"Oh, brother," I said. "God damn it. It's Harry Fellows. God damn it to hell. I thought he'd be safe there in Treasury."

Of course, with that to go on, my mind started putting things together.

"The bald guy's Senator Barker," I said and looked across the table at Ashman. "I had trouble making him because I had a mental block because an anchorman on tv told me last week he was in a hospital with a surprise cancer they'd come across in a routine operation."

Ashman nodded.

"He's going to die next week, after complications," he said. "They'll bury him in Arlington because he was a marine before he got into politics. That last part is true."

"And now I know the room," I said. "It's just where you'd expect a senator and a Treasury agent to be. It's the Oval Office. And that desk, the one I said got hit by a truck, that's the desk of the president of the United States."

I rechecked the photos quickly because there'd been a tall guy in a pinstriped suit with his face down, but the hair was wrong and he was too thin.

"No, that's not him," said Ashman. "That's not the president. But it might have been, it damn near was. They didn't get him only because his wife threw a fit about something a decorator did wrong with the Lincoln Room and screwed up the schedule. We're covering for it now with a story about a minor fire, because those people got away. They're still out there, and they're too damned dangerous. We need your help, John. We need it bad."

I leaned back and noticed I'd left my weapon lying on the table, so I guessed I was going to come along.

"You mean well, and it's very flattering," I said, "but you don't really need just my help, do you? You need *our* help, mine and a certain other person's help, don't you, George? And this other person isn't getting off his rump and it's driving you nuts to watch him sit and pout and not do it. Am I right?"

"You're right, John. You're very, very right," said Ashman and gave a little frown I'm sure his mother knew. "He won't budge. No matter who asks him to. He seems to have no respect at all for official authority."

I smiled at him, kind of toothy.

"I'm a little that way myself, George," I said. "It's one of the main reasons why the two of us, me and this other fellow you want to lend a hand, got along through all those years."

I stood and picked up the coffee cups and started rinsing them off in the sink while I stared out the window, then I had to sigh because wouldn't you know they had that damned, silly limo cruising down Maple Street like a duck out of water again?

"On the other hand," I said, stacking the cups in the rack to drain, "you people really do need our help."

2

The Barton Towers are where you stay if you're convinced you're really important and you're staying at the Barton Hotel, which anybody who understands anything knows is only a sort of poor man's adjunct to them. The higher your Suite is, and of course nobody staying at the Barton Towers can stay in anything less than a suite, the more important you are—deposed dictators wouldn't be seen getting off the elevators until they'd passed the twentieth floor—and the best of all is saved for the very top floor which is, every square foot of it, the Presidential Suite.

But that is not by any means all that is architecturally standoffish about the suite. It is also so constructed and set up that all its working systems function entirely independently from the rest of the building, from having its very own air-conditioning system on down, and the rumor among people in the hotel security business is that if you tore down the whole fifty-nine other floors of the Barton Towers, those snooty top-floor digs would continued to float high above Manhattan.

The Presidential Suite is where Ashman and his friends had stashed Enoch Bone, and it was pathetic to see how proud the poor simps seemed to be of that when they told me about it in the limo. Of course we all left in the limo since I figured that, as Mr. Bowen of

Elmsville was thoroughly and permanently blown, the folks there might as well see their lovable neighbor depart in style.

"Well, then, of course he's grumpy," I said. "Don't you know Bone considers that place a den of thieves and assassins? Some of the people he hates most in the world either live there and boast about it or would kill to roost there. I'd say you boys really did a swell job of getting off on the wrong foot."

I closed the portfolio of stuff Ashman had given me to study and shook my head, not over the blunder he and his gang had made in housing Bone, though that was bad enough, but over the material I'd just been trying to digest.

Along with the photographs he'd already shown me there were plenty of others, including a lot of background shots of a big rally against violence on children's tv which had involved large crowds of angry people toting banners and posters and marching up and down Pennsylvania Avenue, not to mention the sidewalks. The rally had interfered no end with the initial pursuit, but a careful checking-out indicated it was motivated entirely by a laudable desire to preserve the mental health of the nation's young, and unrelated to the attack.

There were also pages of other photos and little maps of rooms and lots of other data resulting from the investigations of a small army of scientists brought in to study the rubble. None of these things much clarified who had done it, not to mention why, but they did a good enough job of showing how well the attack had been planned and executed, and the size and spookiness of the whole business was only just dawning on me as we pulled within sight of New York.

Nothing the terrorists left behind had so far led anywhere at all; not their shells or bullets or even two of their bodies: a thin, tiny, tough-looking Oriental and a burly, large, tough-looking Caucasian, neither of whose fingerprints, photos, or descriptions seemed to have been registered in anybody's files. These two had died from biting little poison pellets someone had doubtless given them for emergencies just like the one they ran into when they'd been forced into a wrong turning in a White House corridor during an otherwise flawless and totally successful escape, which, by the way, was still so completely unexplained that Ashman told me it had reduced the investigators to actually tapping the walls in a hunt for secret panels.

The limo hadn't quite rolled to a stop at the Barton Towers entrance before the car was wrapped in grim-looking men with wires leading to plugs in their ears and one hand each pushed into their pockets, and this bunch did an expert job of seeing to it that we were over the sidewalk and inside an oversized, art deco elevator as quickly as it could be done without their actually lifting us out bodily and tossing us from one of them to the other like a couple of footballs.

"This next part is up to you," Ashman said, watching the little red dots on the indicator zip up the floors. "Until now I've always thought the stories about his stubbornness were unkind exaggerations, but my guess is you're the only person in the world who can budge the old bastard."

"I know," I said, "so I would suggest you leave me to it, and, by the way, stop calling him names. Let me go in alone and don't bother us until I say to, as we definitely don't need a chaperon. And I'm not guaranteeing a thing, understand that."

We stepped out of the elevator into a hallway with two full-scale chandeliers and no end of fancy wood-work.

"Fit for a king," I said, looking around at all the grandeur. "I'm sure he hated it. Where is he?"

Ashman led the way to one impressive door among

many that differed from the rest only in that there was a marine standing by one side of it. He snapped smartly to attention at our approach, but then I wouldn't have expected anything less of him.

"At ease," said Ashman, and he did.

"I see you shift from civilian to military authority once your operation moves out of the common view," I said, and then I paused with my hand on the door's knob, which I suspected might actually be gold plated. "Wait a minute. Has he eaten anything?"

"Nothing," said Ashman. "He said the menu was appalling, that's the word he used, and then he threw it at somebody. I think he's had a couple of pots of coffee, but that's all."

"That's a day and a half without food; a major strike," I said. "He must be starving. They have a staffed kitchen on this floor; tell them to produce two hearty breakfasts. Now. Tell the chef not to try and fool around with fancy stuff, to keep it classic American simple. Blueberry corn muffins, if he thinks he's up to it, Scotch scones if he doesn't, beaten biscuits after that. But not made from a mix, whatever he does. And no frozen sausages. Have it hot and ready and waiting in as close to ten minutes as possible. Now be quiet."

I turned the knob and went in and closed the door behind me, making as little noise doing it as I could. He heard me enter, of course, but he wasn't going to dignify me by looking in my direction because he figured I was one of them. He was wearing one of those Ivy League professorial outfits, tweedy, with suede leather patches on the elbows, but it was all fresh and pressed and the ascot was perfect; the passing of time had by no means turned him sloppy.

It was exciting to see him again after all these years, and I won't pretend my heart didn't bob right up into my throat, but my God how old he was! I couldn't believe all those new wrinkles; he had to have the all-time world record for wrinkles, and when I took in the knobbiness of his hands and the way his back bent over as he sat there looking out of the window it made my heart squeeze and I was within an ace of feeling sorry for him when he did turn—as I knew he would eventually have to do because curiosity always got the better of him—and I saw those gray eyes on me, still bright and sharp and dangerous if riled, and my little pity fit snickered at itself and popped like a bubble because, of course, he was tough and sharp as ever.

He stared hard at me for another moment while his brows, which had grown into two white tufts, swam close to each other and locked hairs over a particularly deep vertical wrinkle over his nose. Then he blinked and stood, which was a relief because I was wondering if he still could, and, finally, he spoke.

"Outrageous!" he said, and his voice was unchanged, exactly as I'd remembered it, with not a knob or wrinkle in it.

"Yes," I said.

"They brought you here? Dragged you from that silly Elmsville? Is there no end to their presumption?"

"No," I said.

By this time we were shaking hands. Maybe that doesn't sound like much, but Enoch Bone and I have only shaken hands four times, counting this time, during all the years we've known one another, and I have only seen him do it with two other people, once each, so it doesn't come easy to him and we didn't drag it out.

He stood back, looking up at me.

"Of course they sent you here to badger me to pry into this grotesque situation," he said.

"Yes, sir," I said. "I told them I'd try, but that there would be no guarantee. They also blew Mr. Bowen, and I liked being Mr. Bowen."

He nodded and wandered over to the wall of floor-to-ceiling windows which afforded a fine view of a sea of glass-box buildings marching along both sides of Park Avenue.

"I know you did," he said. "It was very American and touching of you to want to be Mr. Bowen, and you have my sympathy on his passing." He turned and glared. "But don't try to blackmail me with his loss."

"It would have been foolish not to make the attempt," I said.

"Quite right," he said. "Now you've done it, what's next? An appeal to my patriotism? I am, after all, a naturalized citizen, so it's an entirely valid ploy."

"I was thinking of bringing up the intellectual challenge," I said.

"Actually I'm currently much involved with the medieval philosopher Dogen and his suppositions on the superiority of the pre-intellectual ground," he said, more than a little smugly. "Another time and you might have got me."

"Returned to basics, have you?" I said. "Well, then, we'll have to wait till you work your way back to Descartes. How about breakfast?"

His head didn't move, but his eyes slid around to look at me.

"That's not fair and you know it," he growled.

"Of course it isn't," I said. "How about it? I'm not asking for any full-scale assault on the thing, just to bat some of the facts back and forth over pancakes. There are a lot of really discussible aspects to this fracas."

He looked down at his toes which he could do, now, because he was no longer fat, which I have seen him be; nor was he thin as a rail, which I have seen him be before, a good while earlier on. Nowadays he appeared to have settled for a statistical average so far as corpulence was concerned; the insurance companies would have been proud of him. He sighed.

"All right," he said. "But this does not in any way represent a serious commitment."

I walked over to the door and opened it. Ashman had been hovering and he came forward but I waved him back.

"Not you," I said, "just breakfast."

A cart with a crisp white linen rolled into the room, pushed by a guy with a thick moustache who was wearing one of the fanciest bellboy outfits I'd ever seen outside of the Cote d'Azur, and the covers on the silver tureens rattled cozily and failed entirely to muffle the cozy smells of bacon and biscuits and other good things, but I didn't pay attention to any of that; I whacked the bellboy good and hard across the chest with my forearm the way they'd taught me to do it in the army, grabbed the handle of the cart with both hands as he staggered back, and pushed it head-on and fast as I could at the big windows.

I'd heard stories of suicidal executives having to spend long periods of time battering away at their office windows with briefcases before they could make a hole big enough in their thermal panes to jump through, but my prayers that the glass in these ones would be the old-timey, breakable variety paid off—they must have been the same early-thirties vintage as the rest of the decor—and the cart burst through them in a highly satisfactory spray of glistening shards and spun out into the air.

I didn't pause to stare after it, I spun around at once, but I was still just a half-foot too late to grab the bright red, gold-braided jacket of the bellboy and stop him from diving out of the window just in time to disappear into the big ball of fire and light which was now flashing out from where the tumbling service cart had been.

"Down!" I shouted, and as I was in the process of diving for the floor I threw a quick glance to the side and was pleased to see Bone had already managed to do the same in spite of his years, so we were both huddled on the carpet when the explosion blew in what was left of those windows, but not with anything like the force it might have done if the cart hadn't tumbled something like three stories below us before doing its thing.

There was the usual pause that takes place after an event of that kind, even in the presence of professionals, and then Ashman and the marines came barreling in, altogether willing to help but too late to do much more than mop up after the event.

3

The second breakfast worked out a little better, particularly after Bone found out the chef on duty was a Scot, as he had firm convictions about that race's superior abilities relative to preparing the sort of morning fodder he enjoys. He felt so good about it, as a matter of fact, that he even let Ashman join us.

"Of course," said Bone to me, buttering his second scone, "you are bursting to tell me how you knew that bellboy was a villain, Weston. You deserve to be, and I freely admit that I am more than mildly curious. But first, allow me to announce officially to you, Mr. Ashman—Weston will have understood already—that this attempt on my life has moved your little problem from the area of an abstract puzzle to that of a personal challenge, and therefore, so far as I am concerned, you may consider me fully committed to its satisfactory conclusion, which is to say the death or prolonged internment of those responsible."

Ashman opened his mouth to speak, but since I figured it was highly possible, if not even likely, he'd blurt out something that might give Bone an excuse to change his mind back again, I cut him off by a wave of the hand and picked the portfolio up from where I'd had it leaning on the chair.

"This gave me the clue, as we say in the detective

business," I said, spreading the portfolio open on the table. "This picture here, to be exact, one of the shots of the demonstration that was being held on Pennsylvania Avenue. Specifically, this face in the picture."

They leaned forward to see where I'd poked my index finger.

"By God," said Ashman, "it's that guy with the moustache!"

"Excellent, Weston," said Bone, and there was a grim tone to his voice because, of course, he'd just seen what I'd spotted when I'd studied this stuff in the limo. Apparently Ashman had never managed to bully him into giving the portfolio a good looking over.

"But how were you so damn sure he was up to something?" Ashman asked. "I mean that was one hell of a bold move you made, to say the least."

"Because of who he is with in the photograph, Mr. Ashman," said Bone. "You see? He is supporting the arm of a thin, stooped man."

"That old guy? But his back's turned, Bone. He could be a whole lot of people."

"It is a back unique in my experience," said Bone. "Once seen, never forgotten. Its head, particularly. Its angle, even more particularly. Observe how it is tilted to one side but still upright on its long, scrawny neck. Doesn't that put you irresistibly, Mr. Ashman, in mind of a swaying snake?"

Ashman stared at the photo while Bone and I locked eyes.

"I thought he was dead," I said. "I thought we'd finally killed him."

"So did I," said Bone. "And burnt him to a crisp to boot. But we thought he was dead twice before, didn't we, Weston? First because of my little struggle with him over the Falls, and then because of our arrangement to have him shot with a large number of bullets while he felt snug and safe in his lair. It is more than a little depressing to realize that the fire started by our altercation in the museum failed to do the job. The loss of the Van Goghs makes it especially exasperating."

"Say, just who is this guy?" asked Ashman.

Bone looked at me and I shrugged.

"Why not?" I said. "Maybe this time someone will listen."

"Very well, then," said Bone, turning to Ashman, "in our last encounter with him he was known as Dr. Michael Madden Hackett. He has a fierce ego, you see, and is partial to academic titles. He was, for instance, no less than a full professor during our premier engagement, and that is how I have always thought of him since and think of him now. As the Professor."

Ashman frowned, stared hard at the photograph, then looked up and shook his head.

"Sorry," he said. "I can't seem to pull him out. I don't think I've ever heard of a Dr. Hackett."

"Hardly surprising," said Bone, "as those in authority were almost never aware of him in any of his incarnations. He was—I am sorry to stay still is—expert in remaining well hidden at the center of his webs." He waved at the portfolio. "This sort of business certainly has his mark on it, though it's exceptionally good, even for him. Also, there are aspects to this business which, though my understanding of it is as yet superficial, seem alien to his methods."

"You think there may be someone else in it with him?" asked Ashman. "I mean someone up to his level, someone he respected enough to let them affect his planning?"

Bone stared very seriously at Ashman.

"You surprise me, sir," he said. "I believe I have seriously underestimated you and I apologize, here and now. You have a mordant imagination and that is an appallingly plausible supposition. Yes, there may indeed be others in it."

He turned and pulled the portfolio to him, studying the photograph, then the one on the facing page, then flipped back and forth through all the other pages showing pictures of the demonstration.

"Have all the faces in the photo of this crowd blown up, Mr. Ashman; use all your tricks of computer rectification," Bone said. "Mr. Weston and I will want a good close look at all of them."

He glanced up at me and I shook my head.

"No," I said. "I didn't notice anybody else, but maybe they were there and just being cuter."

Bone gave the side of his nose a series of little taps to indicate his brain was whirring so fast he could hardly stand it, and then he shook his head in dismissal.

"All right," he said. "That part will have to wait. What about the bellboy? I know there's almost nothing left of him proper, but have you come across anything else regarding him? Some leavings?"

Ashman nodded, then turned and raised a hand and the marine who had been standing inside the door—they'd added a second, interior one since the business of the bomb—stepped forth smartly and handed him an envelope.

"He got into the working area of the hotel by wearing the uniform of a parcel carrier," he said. "We're checking out the firm, but I'm pretty sure it was just another trick outfit, and of course we're having the uniform combed over. This was found in the shirt pocket. It doesn't make any sense to us, but maybe it will to you."

Out of the envelope he took a flat plastic sack containing a bright little folder, all spread out with both sides visible.

"Look it over, only please leave it in its protective wrapping. We want it untouched for the lab boys."

He put it on the table and Bone and I hunched over the thing.

"Good grief," Bone gasped, studying it with more or

less the same expression of shock an ordinary man might wear while looking over a color folio of Jack the Ripper's victims. "Weston, what *is* this dreadful place?"

"It's Waldo World," I said. "It's where you take your children if they've been very good and you love them. People cross the continent to do it. They come from foreign lands."

Bone pointed indignantly to the photo of a huge sculpture proudly displayed in the center of the pamphlet's opening fold.

"And this extraordinary object?"

Ashman sat up even a little straighter than usual, staring in shocked disbelief first at Bone and then at me.

"He doesn't know?" he said.

"He doesn't know," I said. "He's led a sheltered life. Only murderers."

Ashman cleared his throat and then turned a palm at the picture of the hundred-foot-high plastic duck, which all the world but Enoch Bone and maybe some undiscovered Amazonian Indians knew, standing on its huge, golden base just within the gates of Waldo World, across the Hudson in New Jersey, waving a welcoming wing at the throngs of incoming customers, and opening and closing its beak in time to the "Lucky Duck" song.

"It's Quacky," Ashman said. "Quacky the Duck."

Bone winced at the sound of the name both times Ashman made it.

"He's an animated cartoon character," I said. "Created back in the early thirties by Art Waldo. He also made up the Pirate Parrots, the Elegant Elves, and I won't go on naming them because I see it's making you sick, but they formed the basis of Waldo Films, Inc., which turned into Waldo Productions, Inc., which has become one of the biggest and most successful Inc.s in the country. I'm afraid finding this pamphlet in the bellboy's pocket ties them all into the case."

There was a little silence except for Bone breathing audibly through his nose, which is one of his more emphatic ways of indicating irritation, and then Ashman cleared his throat again, which was coming across as one of his ways of indicating extreme nervous tension.

"There's something written in some funny language on the other side," he said. "We're going to have our linguistic people study it, but you might as well have a look."

Bone flipped it over.

"It's Romanian," he said. "You won't have to bother your linguists for a simple translation, Mr. Ashman. It says, succinctly: 'Memorize map.' There is also a little mark, a neat *x*, at the intersection of, I am sorry to say, Walter the Whale Way and All-American Avenue. I am afraid you are right, Weston, and that this is unavoidably pertinent and that we must look into it, however distasteful it may be."

"It looks that way, sir," I said.

"Very well, then," said Bone. "I can, for the nonce, by his appearance, tentatively accept our ersatz bellboy as a Romanian, but the lack of a necessary accent and the abruptness of the inscription lead me to at least wonder whether the writer is also a Romanian, and I will be curious to learn, Mr. Ashman, if your linguists share in my suspicions."

He turned my way and gave me a long, sympathetic look.

"I deeply regret inflicting this on you, Weston," he said, "but I'm afraid I must ask you to visit this horrible place and give it a thorough looking over," he said. "Paying particular attention, of course, to the absurd intersection marked on the map."

"One does what one must, sir," I said and turned to Ashman. "Can you set me up as a reporter doing a cover story on Art Waldo for *Folks' Magazine*? That ought to make me enough of a VIP to get access to just about anything there without alarming any potential assassins lurking in Ducky Nests and Elf Castles."

"Sure," said Ashman. "Who knows? Maybe they'll even give you a Golden Duck pin! I entered a contest for one of those when I was a kid, but all I got was a consolation prize, a crumby little picture of Waldo which I tore up and later wished I hadn't. Of course my heart was broken. Will you loan me yours if you get one? It'd really impress my kids."

"Only if you can sing the 'Lucky Duck' song," I said.

"L-U-C," he said, "Lookie and see . . ."

"K-Y-D," I joined in, "Yessir, by gee—"

"Stop!" said Bone. "This instant!"

So we did.

4

They'd stopped giving out Golden Duck pins a long time ago—say about when Ashman had reached seventeen—and taken to handing out little plastic cards like everybody else, so his heart would be broken again; but I *did* get a badge with Quacky's picture on it, big as life, reading "Honored Guest," and figured one of his agency's passport technicians could bleach my name off the thing and forge his in its place and that way his kids would respect their dad.

The card, along with a big, bright, duck-yellow bag full of pamphlets and folders was pressed on me along with a hearty handshake from the large, muscular hand of Frank Nealy, the head of Waldo World's public relations team. Nealy was going gray and bald, on the short side but built broad, like a bouncer, and he'd worked up quite a sweat waiting for me by the gate—I didn't think they'd fool around with a cover story in *Folks'* for bait—in spite of his seersucker suit.

"Hi, there, Mr. Bowen," he said, as I'd decided to give Mr. Bowen of Elmsville a trip to Waldo World as a last treat before he expired completely, "the arrangements we made on the phone are all set: You're going to take the quick tour, though I want you to feel absolutely free to come back anytime you feel the need for a longer one, and then you'll have lunch with Mr. Waldo.

Mr. Waldo is a great admirer of *Folks'*, you know, and mighty pleased at your interest!"

Nealy was a good PR man because he left no doubt at all I was the most important person in the world and that his life was complete now that he'd met me.

"Here's our very own Quackycart, Mr. Bowen," he said, leading me over to a duck-shaped vehicle with a polka-dot awning, "and a VIP Quackycart, no less. Our driver and guide will be Debbie, here, because she's one of our best."

I realized asking for Debbie's last name would be a serious breach of etiquette, and so I just gave her a bright smile back as she snapped me a smart salute off the duck bill of her Quackycap, which I learned could be bought, in a slightly tackier version, at any of the many stores and boutiques in Waldo World. I, of course, had one in my big yellow bag already, being a VIP.

Debbie was a tiny blonde with tennis legs and very cute; not cute like the little forest animals that helped Goldilocks in the famous animated movie of the same name, not cute like the harmless little squirrels and chipmunks and chickadees; Debbie was cute like one of Waldo's more dangerous small cartoon animals such as Flicky the Bat, who the Witch liked in *Rapunzel*, or the mean baby wolf in *Red Riding Hood*. Debbie was like one of Waldo's loveable little predators. I couldn't have told you how I knew all that, I just did.

She got us settled and seat-belted in no time, and while our electric motor was purring us smoothly through a river of kids with their grown-ups, all stuffing themselves with candy and melting ice-cream bars and fast food, all of them party bright with their brand-new banners and hats and huge, stuffed Waldo World toys, she told us about how tall Quacky's statue is and pointed out the parrot skull-and-crossbone flag flying from the top mast of the Pirate Galleon, and I got the strong impression she was, at the same time, listening to everything we said and watching all we did, so for her benefit, and Nealy's, and for anybody else who might be curious, I took out a notebook and scribbled in it now and then; as a good reporter should.

This was my very first trip to Waldo World as I am not a father or an uncle or even a family friend, and I remember writing some pretty gushy things like, "Never saw so many towers!" and "Giant Cheese even better than on tv!" so I had a fine time, but there were a number of things I didn't mention in the notebook, such as that it was difficult at first glance to make any obvious connection between the corner of Wally the Whale Way and All-American Avenue and those nine bloody bodies in the White House, and that Debbie had a neat little holster under her pretty Quackycoat, and that someone in an Ol' Doc Stork suit always seemed to be somewhere in the crowd within sight of us no matter where we went.

We ended our tour with a trip through the ride of my choice, and that was The Old Hollow Oak because I thought it would particularly irritate Bone, and I couldn't wait to see the expression on his face getting worse and worse as I told him about the field-mouse burrow in its roots, and Owl's hollow in its trunk, and the squirrels' branch huts, and the birds' nests in the leaves with baby robins coming out of their little blue shells.

Lunch was in a very private, very Gothic dining room on top of the Wizard's Tower in Elf Castle. It had high walls of what might have been stone and big, dark beams which could have been carved out of ancient oak, though almost nothing in Waldo World was made out of what it seemed to be, and they supported a frescoed ceiling showing a dark blue sky full of constellations of golden stars fixed, I was told, in the exact position they held when Waldo first thought of Quacky the Duck.

Tapestries with scenes from Waldo's most famous movies woven into them hung from each corner, and there were terraces on all four sides from which you could see all of Waldo World without any of Waldo World seeing you because of all the gargoyles in between, and Nealy was showing me that secret view when Art Waldo showed up.

He looked just like he had in the hundred or so pictures I'd seen of him, only maybe a little older than the last set. He was short but hefty, and had a huge head covered with shaggy, iron-gray hair except for a round bald spot on top, just like a good friar in a fairy story, or maybe the imp. He spoke in a voice which was pleasant in spite of being high-pitched and slightly squeaky, paced a lot when he was on his feet, and waved his little bird-claw hands more when he was sitting down, I guess to compensate for the lack of action.

The only sad part about him were his big, heavily tinted glasses, which reminded you about the grisly vision problems that had plagued him since he'd had an accident as a kid and that threatened eventually to blind him entirely, in spite of the numerous medical wonders with which a small army of the world's most expensive eye specialists had attempted to help him.

The food was good, if a little picturesque. Everything was named after some character or place in a Waldo production, and I could hardly wait to tell Bone about the Dismal Swamp Pea Soup which featured little green alligator croutons and even smaller white ones that looked like tiny, floating skulls.

Waldo was, as reporters say, a good interview, telling lots of interesting stories and telling them well in a style that floated back and forth from enthusiastic to dreamy, and we covered a lot of ground, starting out with Waldo World, then going on to the movies that built it, and by dessert we'd worked our way all the way back to where it all started.

"I'll never forget it," he said, leaning back in his golden throne at the head of the table and gazing up at the stars on the ceiling. "Never. It's one of those memories you can call up crystal clear. I was sitting on the porch of the farmhouse because I'd done the afternoon chores, and that gave me Pa's permission for an hour's doodling and dreaming, and I saw that duck waddle across the barnyard in the bright, Kansas sun, and as I watched I saw—I swear it, I actually saw it, it wasn't anything at all like making something up—I saw a little, pointy, green hat appear in the air and settle down on its head, and then, just like that, it was wearing a checkered coat with big, brass buttons."

He smiled and took a long pull at his iced tea through a straw with the pirate flag on it without once looking down.

"And then I heard him talking, Mr. Bowen," he said. "And it was Quacky talking in Quacky's voice. But at the same time it was me talking. Eleven-year-old me."

"And what were you saying, Mr. Waldo?" I asked.

He looked straight at me.

"We were saying, 'Here I am, everybody! Here I am!'"

He smiled and stood and then we all stood, too, just like you do when a judge stands in his court or, I suppose, just like you do when a king stands in his castle. After a moment of silence on all our parts, he turned and wandered out onto the terrace, walking in a kind of a trance.

He'd been using Quacky's voice when he'd quoted the duck. He was, of course—always—Quacky's voice in the movies. It was a firm rule in Waldo Productions,

Inc., I had heard. His smile, just then, had had a lot of Quacky in it, too. I stared after him.

"You're very lucky, Mr. Bowen," said Healy. "Mr. Waldo doesn't often tell that story. You're a very fortunate man."

"I'm impressed," I began, "I'm very impressed."

But then I heard Waldo talking out on the terrace, apparently to me, so I joined him.

"And over there," he was saying, and I have to admit what I heard next really brought me up, "over there we'll put the White House."

"The White House?" I said.

"Yes," he said, turning to me. "You're the first to know, Mr. Bowen. It just recently came to me that we've created enough American Presidential Waldobots to hold an exhibition on their own, and it wouldn't be any problem at all to fill whatever gaps that might create in History Hall, since we've accumulated a regular crowd of backups. Why, we've got all the Academy Award winners Waldoboted in storage, just to give you one example!"

Of course I knew about History Hall with its robot lookalikes, called Waldobots, of the famous and infamous of now and then. You and the kids passed a caveman creating fire at its entrance, and an astronaut putting his foot on the moon at its exit, and in between the family might see just about anybody who was or had been anybody, all of them moving and talking, from Columbus planting the flag, to Dillinger being gunned down by G-men, to the Beatles at their prime.

I'd seen just one Presidential Waldobot, the first one: George Washington. It'd been on special display during a tour some years ago on its unveiling, and I'd only caught a look at the thing because I'd been shadowing a serial murderer who had taken his kids on a day off to see it, and though it was only a computerized contraption with its hands and head covered with plastic skin and the rest of it with a padded period costume, you could almost have believed it was old George himself, if you hadn't looked close and seen the goose-quill pen didn't quite touch when he signed the Constitution.

But Waldo had perfected George and then gone on to build all the rest of them who were important enough to memorize in school, and now they were all on display at History Hall, and if you were in fourth grade and your teacher heard your folks had taken you to Waldo World and you hadn't insisted on improving your mind by viewing the Waldobots, you'd be in trouble when it came to grade time, so Waldo's idea was rock solid because when the Presidential Waldobots made their move there wouldn't be a school kid in the country who would dare skip badgering his parents to pay to visit the mechanical chiefs of state in their brand-new White House, doubtless full-scale, which would sit on what was now a New Jersey marsh.

"Would you like to see our newest Waldobot, Mr. Bowen?" he asked, turning to me with a bright smile. "It's President Parker, and we've just finished him off!"

I told him I definitely would, so the two of us left the top of the Wizard's Tower by means of an elevator concealed in a buttress, and when we got out on the ground floor, Waldo pressed the beak of a tiny gargoyle of Quacky, mounted at the junction of the low ceiling and the opposite wall, and a swell secret panel opened on a large wardrobe closet filled with costumes representing at least twenty different cartoon characters. Waldo leaned forward, selected a Phil the Phantom suit, and began to slip it on.

"I always wear one of these outside," he said. "Otherwise I'd never get anywhere for signing autographs, but it just generally makes it easier to get from place to place. Want to try one?"

I tugged a few sleeves and turned a few masks and the next thing I knew I had taken out and was holding what looked to be the very same Ol' Doc Stork suit I had been catching glimpses of all that morning.

"Yes," I said, "you bet I would."

And he was right, it did make it easy getting around; the crowds parted for you respectfully, no questions asked, and all you had to do in return was wave back to an occasional kid and say something nice, which I did because I have a pretty good Ol' Doc Stork voice and this was the first chance I'd had to use it professionally, and because I was in a pretty good mood since this expedition seemed to be making some really interesting connections.

Eventually Waldo led the way into a dark, dank little garden that ran along the wall of an otherwise sunny Olde English cottage, explaining that his crowd-flow experts had designed the garden's placement so that hardly anyone ever thought to wander into it, and his landscape people had seen to it that those who did would get the creeps and quickly wander out. He went to a wall, pushed one beam and then another in a tricky way, and we stepped through another secret panel into a stark-looking hallway with hospital-green walls, a black, soundless floor, and a ceiling made up entirely of fluorescent panels.

"Quite a contrast," I said. "Aren't you afraid the public will sneak through some of these hidden entrances of yours?"

"They're not easy to open even if you do find them," he said, and then he pointed to tiny television cameras mounted on swivels on either side of the entrance. "And they're all very closely monitored. Besides, secrets are a lot more fun if there's a little risk concerned, and you wouldn't be in your business if you didn't enjoy risks, would you, Mr. Bowen? This way, please."

We headed down the corridor, took one of two identical branches, did that again a little further along, and finally found ourselves in front of a stainless-steel door with an oversized brass handprint set into its middle.

"It reads palms," said Waldo, placing his hand on the brass shape, and, as a sort of low thrum sounded from somewhere, the steel door glided upward out of sight and then glided back down again after we'd stepped through it into a huge room which continued the same kind of grim but efficient decor the hallways had set, but added plenty of extra detail in the way of shelves and counters and banks of computers and numbered storage cabinets along its walls.

I took all this in with a sweep, but then my eyes went to and remained fixed on a group of ominous sheeted tables, the sort you see in a morgue, neatly arranged in marching formation at the room's center. A very tall, very thin man wearing a surgeon's smock and wrap-around dark glasses was curved over the head of the table nearest us, firmly and intently doing something to whatever was under the sheet, but he looked up as we entered and carefully covered his work as we approached.

"I want you to meet our Dr. Schauer," said Waldo. "Doctor, this is Mr. Bowen, from *Folks*'. He's going to do a story on us, and I thought he might like to meet President Parker. Is he in shape for an interview with the press?"

Dr. Schauer gave us a *V*-shaped smile with nicotine-yellow teeth which made his face even more like a shiny, pink skull than before, but he didn't straighten up like I'd expected him to and I realized the sharp arching of his spine was permanent. He reached one rubber-gloved hand over his back and up to give his white hair a perfectionist's pat, though the stuff didn't need it since it was already plastered so tight to his scalp it looked smooth and shiny as a cyclist's helmet.

"Ach, zo—yess, yess, most zertainly!" he said, making a little bob of a bow which brought his pointy chin down even closer to the table and aimed his angular grin directly at its head. "Are you not, my Leader?"

Then he glanced up and gave us a cute little wiggle of his brows as something began stirring under the sheet.

5

"First, its hand came into sight," I told Bone, spreading some butter on a slice of the bread we'd had sent in in order to shame the papier-mâché variations they served in the Barton Towers. "It reached out from under the sheet and took hold of the upper edge. And the thing was, I knew it was *his* hand. Not just the ring, though they had that perfect, but the way it was built, the way it moved."

"How did this Dr. Schauer operate it?" asked Bone. "You haven't mentioned any control panel or microphone or such."

"That's because there wasn't any," I said. "I don't know how they did it, but the effect was that the thing worked without outside instructions."

"Perhaps it was monitored from a distance."

"Perhaps," I said. "Whatever, it pulled the sheet down and there was its head, President Parker's head, smiling up at me with the big, deep dimples and the crinkly, friendly eyes, the way it does at all of us from newspapers and tv screens, and then it pulled the sheet down to its waist—it was wearing a completely unwrinkled pinstriped suit, and I don't know how they did that either—and it sat up and put out its hand and said, 'How do you do, Mr. Bowen? I'm Pat Parker, President of the United States of America, and I'm pleased to meet you!' I suppose it overheard my name from the introductions."

"Bizarre," said Bone, after carefully swallowing a sip of tea. "Obscene. It was truly, credibly like the president?"

"Truly, credibly," I said. "And even more so when it got off the table and stood tall, when you got a clear shot at the whole length of it, and just then I almost said 'him' instead of 'it.' I didn't know whether to pinch it or myself."

"Could it walk around, or was it anchored?" asked Bone.

"Good question," I said. "It was fully mobile. All the previous Waldobots are locked to their platforms, but the Parker model is a whole new departure in plastic historical figures and can go where it wants, even up and down stairs. Everybody in Waldo World is very proud of it."

Bone frowned, brooding.

"I suppose we'll end by having one of the things elected to office," he said.

I turned and reached down and started fishing in the bright yellow VIP bag resting by my chair.

"Dr. Schauer is a great one for backups and he had a lot of spares around, just in case any of the greats of history gets into trouble," I said. "He keeps them filed in drawers and floating in tanks. Extra heads, extra eyes. All very spooky."

I pulled out a human hand and waved it at Bone.

"This is a Dwight D. Eisenhower extra, for instance," I said. "Got a nice tan. From golfing, I suppose. They gave it to me as a souvenir."

I pushed a button on the stub of the wrist and the hand's fingers made a claw at the air.

"Good heavens, how horrible," said Bone, but after staring at it a little longer he said, "then again, it's quite good. Let me have that thing for a moment."

I passed it to him and, after just a little experimentation, he used it to tear off a piece of bread and carry it to his mouth.

"A redundant bit of apparatus if one has one's own hands," he said, chewing in a pleased way as he passed the hand back to me, "but it would be extremely useful if one did not. Most amusing, all the same."

"So there's a presidential connection between the business in Washington and Waldo World," I said, letting the hand drop back into my VIP bag, "but whether it's coincidence or synchronicity or a deep, dark plot is more than I can say. So far."

Bone leaned back with that smug look which always alerts me.

"That is not the only element in the report you've given me tonight which indicates yet another potential connection, Weston," he said. "Remember our being told that, when last heard of, the investigators at the scene had been reduced to verifying whether there might actually be secret panels and passageways in the White House walls? Absurdly, they paid off. They are there, up to and including a tunnel under the Rose Garden which leads to an outside sidewalk."

I snorted.

"Who put them in," I asked, "Thomas Jefferson or Herbert Hoover?"

"They seem to be of considerably more recent vintage," said Bone. "The whole business was probably constructed within the last twelve months, since the first false wall was apparently set up during a now highly suspect repair job of a year ago. Then, working both ways from that initial point of concealment, the builders established an involved network connected with entrances and exits so brilliantly camouflaged by trompe l'oeil painting and illusionistic carpentry that the legal inhabitants, presumably preoccupied with weighty affairs of state, never managed to notice a one of them."

"And they did it all without tripping one single alarm or alerting any guard?" I asked.

"We are up against an organization of surreal ingenuity, Weston," said Bone, tapping his fingertips together contentedly. "A highly satisfying lot, altogether. They appear to be the most extraordinary opponents we have ever met. I am, of course, delighted."

He looked at me, smiled, and rubbed the side of his nose.

"And now what is the little bonbon you've been holding back?" he asked me, raising one brow. "Your hand has approached and withdrawn from your left coat pocket no less than five times during our conversation, so your obvious high hopes for it waver. Trot it out, whatever it is."

"Probably it's nothing at all," I said. "But it does give me a tingle."

"By and large," said Bone, "I have learned to trust your tingles."

I tossed a paper matchbook on the table and Bone's hand picked it up on a sweep, like an owl grabs a mouse.

"Le Rond-Point," he said, reading the raised gold lettering on its maroon front flap. He turned the matchbook around, saw nothing but an address and telephone number, then opened it, and read the inscription penciled inside. "JL 22 XII & ½."

He leaned back.

"July the twenty-second, twelve-thirty," he said. "A luncheon appointment. Two days ago. Why are you interested in this bauble?"

"When I was pretending to be Ol' Doc Stork at Waldo World I slouched around with my hands in the pockets of my Ol' Doc Stork patchwork vest a lot because that's the way he walks in the cartoons and I always like to throw myself into a role."

"Commendable," said Bone. "I see. And this matchbook was in one of the pockets, and someone wearing what might have been that same costume had been keeping you under surveillance during your morning tour of Mr. Waldo's grotesque establishment. Promising, coupled with your tingle. And, even more promising: Have you noticed, Weston, that the ink, pen, and penmanship of this writing is identical to that of the Romanian jotting on that silly map? I see you have not. Enjoy your lunch."

I'd timed my reservation so I'd be dining with the late group, those who either don't have to get back to anywhere on time, or don't have anyone there who would dare to look at them cross-eyed if they did, and they were perfect for the place: too rich and too thin ladies; slick, dominant executives of both sexes in working pinstriped suits; a scattering of smug, very expensive professionals, and a regular crowd of those scary, fragile-looking old money types with cold, confident eyes and odd hairdos, who only go to the right sort of places. There were a few visible celebrities—it's hard to keep them out—but they were all the nonembarrassing types, and they kept themselves carefully muted.

The food at Le Rond-Point had the reputation of being pretty good, especially since they'd gone to the expense of bringing Chef Henri Tomas over from Paris to oversee the operation, but it was mostly famous for its prices, which gave the clientele a chance to impress one another with platinum cards or large, old-fashioned wallets full of bills. As if all that weren't more than enough, the restaurant's table-seating technique was probably the cruelest in the city and considered by experts to be an almost sure fire way to find out it you mattered at all to the people who really counted.

By the time I'd ordered my lunch and was doing what I could with the Terrine of Rabbit Madeira I realized I'd seriously underestimated how much I'd have to tip someone in order to get reasonably accurate information and was wondering if I'd brought enough in spite of the fact that I'd brought a lot, when I caught a cringe and a guilty look out of the corner of my eye, saw it was coming from the new maître d' taking over from the first shift, and knew that my problems were over because he could doll up in a black tie and a waiter's tux and wax his moustache all he wanted, but he was still Frenchy Verne to me, and he knew it.

I smiled at him and he wilted back as I continued my lunch with an increased appetite. The Sole in Saffron Cream Sauce, for example, went down without the slightest trouble, because now I knew that if there was any information to be had I would get it, and for a fraction of what I'd started to plan on forking over. If I'd been in a mean mood, which I wasn't, I had more than enough on Frenchy to get anything I wanted for free.

I didn't rush, I even dawdled so that by the time I'd worked my way through a second cup of coffee and paid the bill the place was practically empty. I rose in a leisurely manner and strolled over to where Frenchy was waiting for me by his little pulpit with the open reservation book lying on top.

"How's it going, Frenchy?" I asked.

"It was going pretty good, Mr. Weston," he said.

"Don't worry," I said. "I won't hurt. I'll even give you a tip. I just want you to run over the customers who showed up for lunch a half-hour after noon on Tuesday and tell me what you know about them, especially the ones who turn out to be interesting to me."

He looked at me for a moment in silence.

"I knew it," he said. "I knew there'd be a follow-up on those guys."

"Tell me about them, Frenchy," I said. "All you can remember."

"Who can forget anything about people like that?" he asked me. "The first one, the old Limey; he wore high-button shoes! You ever seen high-button shoes on anyone? I never seen high-button shoes on anyone, but I knew right off that's what they were the second I seen them. High-button shoes."

"How come you were looking at the old Limey's shoes?" I asked.

"It's one of your basic maître d' tricks," he said. "Guys cover up pretty good on everything else but their shoes; the last thing they know to spend that extra couple hundred bucks for is shoes, so that's where we look if we're checking them out. And this guy had high-button shoes. And they were old. My God, they were old. But he kept them up, you know? Nice polish. And his clothes, pepper-and-salt tweed, only greenish. They was kept up nice, too. But old. Everything about this guy is very old. And it feels damp and cold standing next to him, like there was a draft coming from somewheres, only don't ask me how he did that."

He held a hand up about a half foot over his own head and studied it.

"That's him, around here, almost six feet, in spite of being a little bent over," he said. "And skinny. And bald. And pale. Bluish pale, and dark purple around the eyes like he'd painted the pits with ink. Very bright, very mean eyes, Mr. Weston, so please don't ever tell him I told you anything about him, okay? Because one look from those eyes and I gave him a table maybe five times better than the one I'd figured on giving him before."

He bent over his appointment book, ruffling back the pages.

"Here he is, Dr. Hackett, no first name, party of two, request for quiet table; called in a day ahead so it was

Hugo took it down instead of me." Frenchy stared at the page, tapping it slowly. "He had a funny way of moving his head from side to side while he watched you, you know? Like some kind of a goddam cobra is what it was. So I took him to table nineteen."

We walked slowly over to table nineteen. There was just one couple left in the place, over to one side. They were laughing, they sounded a little drunk, and the man was settling up with his captain. All the other staff had faded away except for one pudgy little guy in a red jacket waiting to reset the table after the couple left. Frenchy rapped the fresh, white tablecloth of table nineteen softly with his knuckles.

"It's a good table, one of the best. I was crazy to sit this Dr. Hackett here but he scared the shit out of me is what it was. Mrs. Forsythe was sitting here to his left along with Miss Pockett; she takes care of Mrs. Forsythe who needs care because sometimes she kind of gets out of control and breaks things and uses language from when she was very young, and Mr. Kepler and Mr. Blaine were sitting here to his right talking lawyer stuff, and he's facing the Hendersons' table where they're having their daughter in from boarding school. Of course all these people spot him right away and they're all pissed off at me for putting this weird, scary old man in the middle of them, at one of the best tables in the place, but it's too late, I've done it.

"'Bring me a neat Irish whiskey, a double,' he says, looking up at me with that swaying head of his. 'My friend, Mr. King, will be arriving shortly. Have some tea brewing for him as he will want it very, very dark the exact instant he arrives. He is a Chinese gentleman, you see.' And then he smiles, like he's explained something to a little kid."

Frenchy turned and stared at the entrance.

"So I fixed all that up with his captain, who could also kill me along with Mrs. Forsythe and the lawyers and the Hendersons, and I'm heading back to my station when I look up and see his friend come in—and there is no doubt in my mind from the first glance that it is his friend, because my heart practically stops when I get a look at him—and I won't say the place goes entirely silent, but practically, because the friend is only a little bit under seven feet tall, all right? And thin like a skeleton. *Like a skeleton*, Mr. Weston, I'm not giving you any figure of speech, here, with a face to match, like a goddam skull, I kid you not, hollows under his cheeks you could put oranges in, and his eyes are green and shine the light back like a cat's, I swear it to God, and he gave such a look down at me with those eyes at the start that I never dared meet his face again, and he's wearing this goddam black robe with a gold dragon running down its front and a black cap with a little red ball on its top, and I've got to walk this horrible person, this creature like something your mother made up to frighten you with because you've been a bad boy, I've got to walk him into Le Rond-Point as a customer, Mr. Weston!"

Frenchy looked up, got strength from somewhere, and went on.

"We got particular clients, Mr. Weston, very particular, the kind of people you've got to hop around if you're going to keep them happy, and they're the kind you have to keep happy, Mr. Weston, you really do, because these people take themselves really seriously, you've no idea how seriously they take themselves. They're dangerous, Mr. Weston, you don't fool around with people like this, believe me, you don't spoil their party."

Frenchy paused and took the neat, squared hankie out of the pocket of his tuxedo and got it mussed patting at his forehead as he watched the memory of himself walking Mr. King from the entrance toward table nineteen.

"So I figured, there goes my job, but what can I do? Because this guy scares me more than the first one did, so I'm walking the Chinaman in, and then," he paused and looked at me, "and then I see it happening. These people here," he paused again and waved around at the empty room, "I see them staring at him; first they're surprised, and then they're angry, and then—and this is what I hadn't expected, see?—all their eyes got big, see? Like little kids, bulging out of their sockets with the whites showing, and they all pulled back from the tables and pressed against the backs of their chairs. They're cringing, see? And it comes to me all of a sudden that these people here are scared of him, too, Mr. Weston, that maybe they're even more scared of him than I am, probably, because they *know*, because they're *experts* in being bastards, see? They're world class! So they know, better than maybe any other crowd you could get together, that he is worse than they are, and what that means if you follow it through is that *he is the worst there is!*"

He dabbed at his brow once more, then noticed the rumples he'd made in his handkerchief by doing it and carefully smoothed them out before returning it to its pocket.

"And that's it," he said. "No more trouble. Everybody pretends that none of it ever happened and they leave the two of them alone from then on without a single other look at either one of them. It's like they all signed a kind of a pact, all these people. The two guys had their lunch and talked over whatever it was they talked over and left and nobody's brought them up since. Except now, for you."

"Did you hear anything they said, Frenchy?" I asked.

He looked at me wide-eyed and shook his head.

"I never went near the table again, Mr. Weston, believe me. The only staff that went near them was their captain and his staff, and once M'sieur Tomas stopped by and chatted with them for maybe five minutes, but I don't know what about. It looked like something complicated. Probably it was something about the food, some bitch or some rave about the sauce, or how this or that isn't as good as the one they had somewhere else, or how it's better. That's what the clients usually talk about with M'sieur Tomas. Okay? So that's it. That's all I know."

Then he frowned and looked into space.

"There was something the old Limey did," he said. "Before he came in the dining room, before I saw him. He left two shopping bags with the girl in the checkroom, just like an ordinary person—crazy, right?—and they weren't the sort of shopping bags you'd figure a guy like that would carry, if you figured a guy like that would carry shopping bags at all; one was from Waldo World, for God's sake, where the duck is! And the other was from Athenee, the jewelers. Suzie couldn't believe it. She said—"

Frenchy's eyes froze looking over my shoulder and then went back to me.

"And now I see M'sieur Tomas has returned, so I'd really appreciate it if you wouldn't mind leaving, Mr. Weston, because if you hang around it'll look like we're talking too much and I'd have to try a lie on M'sieur Tomas and he sees through the damn things every time."

"It must make it hard, being a headwaiter," I said, visibly handing him some folding money during a handshake good-bye, both because he'd earned it, and because that's what customers do to maître d's who've done a good job and it would probably help Frenchy's standing a little if Tomas saw me doing it.

I headed for the entrance and saw M'sieur Tomas had planted himself by its side and was giving the once-over to the latest entries in his reservation book. He was distinguished-looking, I'll hand him that, but the black of his hair was far too deep and flawless for his age, and in my opinion he overdid the haughty carriage number, carrying his head and shoulders as high and proud as if they were a brass bust of Napoleon.

He gave me just the right amount of nod for someone he'd never seen in his life, and the last I saw of him he was gliding toward his maître d' with a questioning look under faintly raised eyebrows, so it looked as if Frenchy would have to try a lie or two on him after all.

6

I miss phone booths generally and I missed one now in particular because a display of brass and ivory jewelry on the sidewalk was crowding my left foot and a wobbly pyramid of pretend transistor radios was leaning on the right one, and because sticking my head into the funny little box the phone was bolted into wasn't muffling the sound of a passing truck and I could barely hear Bone's voice over the crumby little receiver which was, of course, partially broken.

"In full regalia?" he was saying. "The Mandarin marched into the restaurant in broad daylight in full regalia?"

"Actually, they keep it kind of dark in the restaurant," I said, trying to make myself heard over an argument which had just broken out between a futuristic bicyclist delivering messages and an elderly Wall Street type, "I think it has something to do with wrinkles. Yes, he did. If you'd seen it I bet it would really have taken you back to the old Limehouse days. Frenchy said he had on his cap with the coral ball on top and his dragon robe and the whole damn works, just like he was dolled up for a meeting of the Council of Seven, all of whom, the way it's going, are probably in fine shape instead of drowned in that submarine."

"The audacity of it," said Bone. "The gall! What is

that infuriating ruckus in the background? Never mind. So he's back!"

"Right," I said. "And that makes another big one we didn't kill, after all, and now they're together, so it's worse than before. Life can be pretty unfair."

"I don't like that other business," he muttered.

"The second shopping bag?" I said. "I bet you don't like it, and I don't like it either. I never heard of Athenee's, but in Elmsville we tended to miss out on the news of a lot of swank openings; that was one of the best things about living there. I'm standing across the street from the place right now; it's all big windows framed with shiny, glitzy steel and full of really pretty clothes. It looks very posh, and it takes up the whole ground floor of a little old-timey building, and there's something flickering in an open window on the third—"

I stopped because the little pyramid of radios had suddenly flown apart for no visible reason and the jewelry dealer on my other side had given a funny little hiccup and slumped in his burnoose all over the sidewalk. There wasn't any sound of shooting, just that of the breakage and the dying.

"Get Ashman here," I said, and then I left the phone without further instructions because a large hole had opened up in the telephone's front, once more without the hint of a gunshot, and I started heading across the street toward the building which housed the sniper, as it had occurred to me that since everything else in the area was a potential target, that might be the safest place to be.

I tried to make my path of progress as varied and confusing as I could by cute dodgings and duckings and I used delivery trucks and the cars of suburbanites for cover as much as I could, but that didn't stop interesting patterns of holes and gouges from appearing in the tar directly behind and before me as I moved along, again all of it without any noise at all except for the impacts and rippings, and by the time I'd made my way to the front door of the place, Madison Avenue had taken quite a beating.

Nobody in the store had noticed any of this preamble so it came as quite a big surprise to everybody when I burst through the door shouting things like, "Police!" and, "Where's the stairs?" and there were a number of screams and the usual sort of confusion you've got to expect if you barge into a place waving around a large automatic pistol.

I hurried over to the stairway entrance at the rear of the store, lunged through it, and raced up two flights as fast as I could. I was lucky enough to reach the third story before the sniper left and that gave him the chance to demolish the section of the wall which had been directly behind me the instant before I'd thrown myself down flat on the steps. Up close like that the lack of any sort of gunshot noise was really spectacular considering the damage, but now that I was this close I could hear a series of little clicks under the cracking and smashing of the wall and woodwork, so I expressed my feelings about that by throwing a number of rounds in the clicks' general direction.

Our combined efforts had the air so full of plaster dust the effect was like a bleached pea-soup fog and since that made us both blind I decided to forge right ahead, sending regular bullets into the white blank in front of me where I kept hearing those clicks, and in no time at all there was a yell and a clatter which did my heart good. Then I heard a faint monkey scuttle I couldn't locate and a bump overhead followed by a shaft of light beaming down like a sunbeam through sandy water, so he'd made it through the roof trap.

I threw a couple of shots that way to discourage lurking, climbed a dinky metal ladder set into the wall, and popped my head into the sunlight just in time to see the tag end of a thin, shiny rope zip up and over the edge of the roof of the next building, two more stories of smooth wall rising up without a handhold from where I stood.

I walked over and patted the bricks here and there for a possible grip on the theory that you never know what will happen if you give it that little extra try, and though this time that didn't work out, I did manage to spot some nice little smears of blood the clicker had left here and there on the way up, and a stroll back to the trap showed me a splotchy little trail of the stuff on the asphalt and gravel of the roof.

Back inside, the air had more or less cleared of plaster, and in the dust that had come down earlier you could see our footprints. Mine were big, and that was no surprise, and his were tiny and thin, but that was no surprise either because I knew that the Mandarin's best scouts and sneak killers had always been small, elastic little bastards who we'd learned could flatten their bodies like rats in order to squeeze themselves into places you'd ordinarily swear were safe.

I heard a clumping and a clatter on the stairs and looked up to see Ashman's bulldog face peering at me over the landing. He and a big guy with a long, grim jaw standing in back of him had their guns out and pointing.

"Good," I said, "you're quick. Do it again and have someone check the building to the north. I wounded the guy and there's a chance he may still be working his way down or even have stopped."

Ashman turned and passed that on to the fellow behind him, addressing him as Paley, and then came up and joined me and that's how the two of us saw the gun and said "Wow!" at the same exact instant.

It was a kind of rapid-fire rifle but with a whole lot of ideas deserving wows, including two circular clips with a double row of ammunition on either side of its firing chamber, and a silencer which looked like a big round ball of sponge rubber and which I knew for certain worked like a charm.

"I've never seen a weapon like this," said Ashman.

"Try going up against it if you want to really appreciate it," I said.

He bent down over it, carefully, not touching a thing, then he gave a nod and a small grin.

"I think this explains a little something that really had us puzzled," he said.

"What was that?"

"You may not have noticed because you were too busy trying to keep alive," said Ashman. "But following your track we noticed there weren't any bullets on the scene. Not one. Lots of damage, lots of holes, but nothing for ballistics. Take a look at these weird tips pointing out of the magazines."

I leaned over his shoulder and saw what he meant. Instead of lead or metal jackets, the bullets were made out of something transparent but cloudy.

"My guess is they self-destruct after doing the damage," he said, "but somebody built them so cute they don't do it before. I can't wait until the lab gets hold of them. Working out their composition must have taken some pretty fancy calculations."

"These are very fancy people," I said. "And they've had years of peaceful retirement to think up new nasty tricks, so be ready for a lot more calculations."

We were halfway down the ground flight when I heard Bone's voice and almost stopped dead on the stairway.

"He's here?" I said.

"We couldn't stop him," said Ashman. "I think he was worried about you."

I opened the door and there he was, decked out in an old checked Inverness cape I'd only seen in photos, and a cane and wide-brimmed hat I remembered seeing many times in person. He turned and all the wrinkles in his face creased into a smile when he saw us.

"I'm glad to observe you continue to be the successful man of action, Weston," he said.

"I can still duck bullets if I have to," I said. "It looks like you've become something of a man of action yourself."

"I have dropped a few affectations of my middle age," he said, "and am quite the gallivanter in my later years."

But by then I'd noticed who he'd been talking to and so I wasn't listening to him anymore, I was looking at her, and I realized, in spite of what I'd said to Bone on the subject, I'd been hoping all along that the name Athenee meant her in spite of the probable complications.

"You still look good," I said. "You're still probably the most beautiful woman in the world."

She smiled and damn it if my chest didn't do what it always did. Her hair was still dark as a heroine's out of Poe, and her eyes still startled me with their blueness, and damn if I didn't blush when I realized she was still wearing the perfume I'd told her I liked back in Algiers.

"I'm glad you got out of that nasty snake pit," she said. "I hated to let him throw you in there, but otherwise he would have killed you."

"I tried to hold it against you for years but could never make it stick," I said. "Besides, you did sneak me the rope."

She looked down, then looked back up.

"I have missed you, John," she said, saying it *Jean*, like she always did. "I tried to find you."

"I put a lot of effort into being hard to find," I said. "There were a number of people I didn't want to find me. Your father, for example."

"Athenee says," observed Bone guardedly, "that she

has not seen or heard from her father since the business in Dahomey."

"It is true," she said. "I was furious with him for what he tried to do to you. But I had to make arrangements before I left him because with someone like my father one always has to make arrangements, even if one is his daughter, *n'est-ce pas?*"

"Or he's liable to kill one," I said. "So now you're a simple businesswoman and all you do is run this classy shop, which is nothing more than the honest, above-board operation it appears to be."

She shrugged.

"It sounds silly, I admit it," she said, but then she lifted her chin and looked me square in the eye. "All the same, it's true!"

Bone sighed.

"I regret raising certain points, mademoiselle," he said. "Forgive me; I am, after all, a detective. What about the recent visit of the extremely unpleasant gentleman who recently called himself Dr. Hackett, but who, I imagine, the three of us present think of still as the Professor? Obviously both you and your father were familiar with his criminal exploits, simple professional interest alone would have dictated that; but I am surprised to learn you are acquainted with him. I had thought up to now that all of your sinister activities were always entirely independent of one another's, that there was no association between you. What was the purpose of his call on your establishment?"

She threw a glare at Bone, one of the old-time glares I well remembered, but he only smiled benignly back like someone's dear old grandfather.

"All right," she said, forcibly composing herself. "So you know about that. Very well, he did come by—my God but he is a hateful creature—only I never met him before. It is the first time in my life I saw him and I hope it will be the last."

She turned and looked at me.

"I swear it, John," she said.

She turned back to Bone.

"He was buying a bracelet, a very expensive one, and made some fuss about it until one of the girls got hold of me," she said. "Of course I knew him from photographs the moment I saw him, the old horror, and he lit up with a nasty grin the moment he saw me. I suppose he was proud of himself for tracking me down. But we only talked about that stupid bracelet. So I think that's all there was to it, really; I think he just wanted to see for himself if I was *that* Athenee, the daughter of Spectrobert."

She paused and looked around at us.

"There it is, then," she said. "I've spoken it—there's the horrifying name that frightened all of France, eh? All the world. I haven't said it in years. It's been nice not saying it."

She shook her head and sighed.

"Anyhow," she said, "once he was positive about his little triumph—I had the little mole on my left cheek removed; you used to call it my beauty spot, John, but I saw him see the scar with his sharp old eyes all right—he took his bracelet and left, the vile old villian, and that's it. *C'est ca.*"

The door of the store opened and Ashman came in, which made me realize I hadn't noticed he'd left.

"You got him, Weston," he said. "You got him good. We found his body on the stairs. I swear I don't know how he managed to climb up that silk rope of his. I thought you might like a look at him, so here's the latest in up-to-date forensics."

He produced a Polaroid shot of a tiny, birdlike dark man wearing a gray kaftan and turban, and I could remember when an outfit like that would have drawn a second look in New York. He was all curled up tight on a dirty, bloody flight of steps in full fetal posture, but he still looked dangerous. I took the photo and held it out to Athenee.

"All right," I said. "I'm a detective, too, so I have to ask. Why were you keeping something like this in your attic?"

"I'm afraid it's a very good question, mademoiselle," said Bone.

"Really," said Athenee, her glare in full force, "I had almost forgotten how tiresome you two can be!"

Ashman looked from Bone to me and back again.

"Say, look, she didn't have anything to do with it," he said. "The guy broke in from the roof; he forced the trap door and busted a weird knife with a wavy blade doing it. Paley says you call it a kris."

Then he studied the expressions on our faces.

"You guys seem surprised," he said.

"Relieved, Ashman," I said. "What you're looking at here, on my face, is relief."

7

Bone and Ashman and I sat in the back of yet another government limo while Ashman's man Paley drove it slowly down Park Avenue because there was no way to move down Park this time of day except slowly unless you let loose with a siren, and the clowns who equipped the car apparently figured a siren would be far too crude for a vehicle this classy.

"That rifleman was in place within a quarter hour of my little chat with Frenchy," I said. "And his being there shows they got everything out of him, down to the detail about the shopping bags."

"It must have been some firm questioning," said Ashman.

"Quite so," said Bone, as we turned into Fifty-fifth Street. "And the answers very much disapproved of. Le Rond-Point is over there, Mr. Paley. To the left, with that modest little awning which is ever a sure indication of gourmet pretensions."

Paley doubled-parked, probably out of habit because he was a government man, and we piled out and then bunched up in a clump at the door because it wouldn't open. There was a little bunch of pale flowers and a handwritten note fixed to the grillwork with a gold and purple ribbon.

69

"A little funeral bouquet," said Bone. "How very Old Country."

"I can't read the note," said Ashman, "because it's written in French."

"A positively insufferable example of restaurant *snobisme*," said Bone. "It informs us that the management is desolate, but the restaurant is closed due to a death in the family."

He cocked an eye up at me.

"This could have its sinister implications, Weston," he said.

"Get around to the back of this place, Paley, and keep an eye on the rear exit," said Ashman and turned to us as Paley hurried off. "I don't have a warrant, of course, but I think you'll agree we have grounds here for a strong suspicion that a crime may be in progress on these premises, am I right?"

"Absolutely, officer," I said.

"Okay," said Ashman, and producing a little wallet with an assortment of fancy metal equipment in it, he had the lock picked and the door opened in nothing flat. An alarm went off, of course, but Ashman fished around, found a switch under a curtain to the left of the door, and flipped it off with the same little kit.

"I don't know why people don't hide those things better," he said.

"Especially master criminals," I said.

The place was dark, so we turned lights on as we went. There's always something slightly spooky about a completely public place, such as a restaurant, when it's abandoned; it just doesn't seem right not to have any of the usual cast around.

"There's a coat hanging in the checkroom," said Bone, so I ducked in to frisk it and came up with a couple of envelopes containing routine bills addressed to an Arnaud Verne.

"It's Frenchy's," I said.

Bone flipped the switches which turned on the chandeliers and table lamps in the restaurant's main dining room. Everything was neat and tidy, all ready for the next serving, but nobody was home. All in all it was a little like coming aboard a really fancy version of the abandoned *Marie Celeste*. Bone frowned and raised his nose and Ashman and I followed suit.

"Something's cooking," Ashman said.

For some reason that was the signal for both Ashman and myself to draw our guns. Bone headed for the kitchen, with us on his heels, pushed open one of the brightly polished swinging doors, and a rich smell of thyme and garlic and meat flowed out with the motion.

"Not a light on in the whole place," he said. "Not one."

"Smells like roast pork," said Ashman. "Really mouth-watering."

Bone reached in and groped around on the wall until banks of lights flickered on, one by one, starting from over our heads and working their way to the far edges of the big room.

"Keep very much on the alert," he said.

His nose lifted like a hound on the trail, Bone walked across the kitchen to one of the largest ovens in a bank of them stretching across the back wall. He looked around, located a large rag, and used it to open the oven. In it was the biggest baking pan I'd ever seen, filled with some huge, hulking thing.

"My God, that smells good," said Ashman.

"I expect I could have handled that some years back," said Bone, "but in my present state of decrepitude it might prove rather too heavy for me to manage. If you two gentlemen will take hold of the rack, one on either side, and pull it out a half foot or so, we'll have a better idea of what we're looking at. For heaven's sake, please do try to avoid pulling it out far enough to tilt it and spill it out onto the floor."

By now I had a fair idea of what we were tugging into view, but Ashman apparently didn't because his expression was only one of mild curiosity until the rack got about a foot and a half out and the front end of the pan was clear of the oven. At that point the look on his face changed dramatically and so did the color of his skin because what we were looking at, all brown and crispy and roasted to perfection, was Frenchy Verne with an apple in his mouth.

There was a brief pause during which, I think understandably, all our eyes were fixed on Frenchy's glistening face, and during that moment someone with a very good sense of timing slipped into the kitchen and turned out all the lights.

"The devil!" snapped Bone.

"At your service, Enoch Bone!"

It was an actor's voice, full and deep and rolling, with a great snarl whipping through the name at the end. I felt Bone start and stiffen in the darkness beside me.

"Spectrobert," he said, putting a lot of sneer into it. "Still up to your usual cheap theatrics?"

There was a soft hiss in the air followed by a sharp clang against one of the ovens in back of us, and I saw a glittering in the air dangerously close to my nose which was followed by a bang and a clatter on the floor.

"Get low," I whispered. "He's throwing chef's knives."

"There's got to be a lot of those in a place like this!" Ashman whispered back.

We'd barely bunched ourselves behind a counter when, one right after the other, like tumblers in a circus, three monster-bladed meat cleavers thunked neatly into the butcher block mounted onto its top.

"Mine landed a little less than an inch from my face," I whispered. "How about yours?"

"The same," said Ashman.

"He's playing with us, the scoundrel," growled Bone.

"He's got one of those infernal gadgets that sees in the dark. Shoot him, Weston."

"I'd love to," I said. "But I bet he isn't where I think he is."

As if to bear me out, there was a sort of metal avalanche at the far end of the kitchen, and then, even before the last clattering of the first died out, another crash and banging sounded at the room's other end.

"Sounds like two train collisions," said Ashman.

"Hush!" hissed Bone. "Listen!"

I could barely make it out for the ringing in my ears, but as I strained to hear it came clearer: a kind of heavy, sloppy gurgling.

"Whatever it is," said Ashman, "it sounds disgusting."

Then from all directions, the stench hit us; it was as if a thick, sour cloud were pouring in at us from every filthy kitchen in the world, and it was growing stronger and more sickening with each breath we took.

I shifted my crouch in a try to peer better into the dimness from where the second clattering had come and would have tumbled to the floor if I hadn't grabbed the counter because my foot had slipped from under me with a kind of cossack kick because it had suddenly lost all traction. I reached down to what had been sparkling clean tile moments before, touched it with my fingers, and found it was covered with a fatty, putrid slime.

"The bastard's flooding the place with grease," I said. "And he's been saving the stuff for years from the stink of it."

Then that big, full actor's voice boomed out of the darkness again.

"Are you enjoying the presentation of our *spécialité* for tonight, Monsieur Bone?" it said. "I most sincerely hope so for I have created it with you very particularly in mind—Detectives Flambés!"

"Get your guns ready," whispered Bone, grimly. "If you have any spares, get them ready, too!"

Then, along the walls of both ends of the kitchen at once, great banks of flame shot up from the floor, licked at the ceiling and started to spread immediately from both directions, sputtering and sparking toward the center, toward us.

"There!" cried Bone. "Look before you! I *thought* he couldn't resist a moment of triumphant visibility!"

Lit suddenly by a blue-green sea of flames from the grease fire, his shadow huge and wobbly behind him on the kitchen wall, Chef Tomas stood before us, his hands clawed out for the doors leading to his restaurant, staring at us over his shoulder with his teeth showing in a wide, fixed grin which made him look like some kind of a demon under his high, white cap. If he'd dived through the door then we might have frozen, it was such a strange, wild kind of sight; but it was he who was frozen.

Ashman and I had our guns ready and we fired at will, which was often, making smoky holes which sprouted red snakes down what had been the spotless white cloth of Tomas's jacket, but I knew at once we'd done very wrong when he jumped and slumped but somehow didn't fall.

Bone stood suddenly, clawing at the counter for support, his eyes flashing, and I never, not in all the years I've worked with him, even discounting how those new deep lines in his face made it look like an Eskimo mask, saw him show such fury.

"You'll pay for this, Spectrobert!" he roared, waving his forefinger wildly in the air. "Mark that, blast you! Be waiting for it!"

I grabbed hold of him because the flames were closer, almost on us, and somehow managed to keep both of us upright as I worked our way through the thick, black smoke, closer and closer to the door, by grabbing the edges of things as they came into reach. Bone ignored all this and continued to howl and rage as I hauled him along.

"I'll avenge him, you scum! Fear my retribution, you wretch!"

"What the hell is all this?" Ashman asked behind me. "The son of a bitch is dead, isn't he? Look!"

He fired another shot into the bloody chef's jacket and the body jerked where it stood.

"Stop!" I said. "Don't do that!"

Now we were next to the corpse, so I shifted Bone to my other side and reached out to the body and tugged hard at its arm.

"Help me get him loose," I said. "We'll have to lift him a little. He's been stuck up here on some goddam meat hooks."

"Jesus!" said Ashman.

We hauled him off the wall and with Ashman lugging the body and me lugging Bone, we pushed our way through the doors and into the restaurant, and the damnedest thing was it still looked so lovely and peaceful out there you almost wanted to sit down for lunch.

"Let's get out of here," I said. "Outside the building. He may have the place mined with explosives, he may have it ready to fill with poison gas. With that creep anything is possible."

Going out, we crossed paths with some firemen in the hallway, so the blaze must have tripped some alarm. Since they'd made it safely inside, and since none of them were turning blue, I figured that was probably that so far as mines or poison gas were concerned, but I didn't blame myself for worrying about such things; not with Spectrobert.

Ashman laid the body on the sidewalk and there, staring up at us, still wearing that weird, broad grin, was the same face I'd seen earlier that afternoon when I thought I was looking at the famous Chef Tomas but was actually looking at Spectrobert in yet another flawless disguise. I bent down close to the face and talked to it as gently as I could what with all the confusion going on around the two of us.

"Sorry," I said, "but if I had this rubbish on, I'd want you to get rid of it for me."

First I tugged out the plastic gadget in his mouth that had held it in that grin, and in the process discovered that the damned thing had served a double purpose as a nasty and efficient gag, then I took a firm hold of the nose, which was made of some rubbery stuff, worked it back and forth to loosen the extensions glued to the forehead and cheeks so I could pull it loose and free it along with the moustache and the better-than-you brows which arched over his eyes, and when I got rid of that and wiped off some other junk, I closed the eyes of the tired, dead, Irish cop face that doing all that had uncovered.

"Paley!" said Ashman, exploding the name and crunching his hands into fists. "The dirty bastard made us kill Paley!"

He stared down at him, taking deep, raggedy breaths, and then he stood, stuffing his hands in his pockets almost hard enough to push them through the cloth and I could see he was well on his way to being as mad as Enoch Bone.

8

Needless to say, everybody had a lot of questions to ask us since all police organizations tend to put top priority on the murder of one of their own, and it was a good thing Bone and I had a member of their agency as a corroborating witness in the business because they might never have really believed us, deep down inside, if we'd charged in there alone and slaughtered poor Paley all by ourselves.

This was my first sight of their new headquarters, since it had been built during my retirement, and I have to say all those escalators running smoothly up and down through floorsful of postmodern interiors created a much snappier impression on a visitor than the old brick pile they used to skulk around in a few blocks further on downtown.

The slick new architecture was only part of the act, however, merely the setting for the bright and shiny high-tech equipment which was built into their new digs and which starred a monster computer lovingly referred to as CLAMP, for Crime Listing and Monitoring Program.

We were gathered in the office of Fred Greyer, Ashman's superior and head of their agency's New York City section. Greyer probably parted his hair with a ruler, and I wouldn't be in the least surprised to learn he'd been born wearing a three-piece suit without a wrinkle in it. I also suspect that deep down in Greyer's heart, he believed that odd people such as Bone, and possibly even myself, should be taken out and shot for being confusing to logical, orderly minds.

Greyer was hunched over a keyboard plugged into CLAMP because one question leading to another had eventually turned all of them into questions about the Professor, the Mandarin, and Spectrobert, and since the machine's big speciality was digging up information on unpleasant people and keeping track of their activities, all of us were very interested to see what the big machine would come up with.

It was easy enough for Greyer to get CLAMP to print a fat, bulky file on Spectrobert; the Frenchman had always loved headlines so much that if he had nothing else going he'd pass the time by writing letters to the newspapers in his trick vanishing ink threatening to steal the Eiffel Tower. But both the Mandarin and the Professor were very private people and the section head had been typing inquiries about the two of them for the better part of three hours without getting much more than a few sketchy little lines of input.

Ordinarily I would imagine Greyer does a pretty good job of giving people the impression he is unflappable and that under his pinstripes there lurks a core of steel, but now he was in the classic position of the man whose favorite puppy dog just stands there in the middle of the carpet and won't do its clever little tricks, and he looked a little flustered.

"With all due respect, Mr. Bone," he said, "I find it hard to believe these other two people could be the towering criminals you say they are and yet make such a small impression on CLAMP. This Chinese fellow, for instance, who you say recently went by the name of, ah, Mr. King . . ."

"Not only his most recent name, Mr. Greyer," said Bone. "I believe I said it has been strongly hinted it may also have been his earliest, back in the London docklands before the war, when he first became known to the Western authorities, excluding, apparently, those supplying information to your CLAMP. It may even be his genuine appellation."

"Be that as it may," said Greyer, "if he's been behind a tenth of the crimes and terrorist activities you've attributed to him in the testimony you've given me today, here in this office, it's impossible that CLAMP wouldn't have a larger body of data on him. I mean it *is* directly connected with the filing systems of every major police force in the free world, and indirectly, so to speak, with those in the communist territories, so he'd just have to turn up more than he has. The same goes for the man you like to call the Professor, Mr. Bone. There's just no way these people could carry on the wide-ranging criminal activities you've described and leave so small a trace."

"As you say, Mr. Greyer," said Bone, "with all respect. But this truly marvelous device of yours is only the extension of a bureaucracy, after all, sir, a sort of concretion of it. When all is said and done what it really does is verify and enhance, not escape from, policedom's previous errors."

Greyer studied him carefully, trying to figure out how badly he and his gadget had been insulted.

"However," Bone continued, using that kindly smile which seemed to have come to him in his old age, "it does strike me that your CLAMP might yield intriguing information if prodded from a new direction. I think I have watched you manipulate the device sufficiently long to be able to operate its keyboard myself, with, of course, your assistance if I make some silly technical gaffe. Would it be presumptuous of me to put a few questions to it directly?"

Greyer stared at him for a moment, and then shrugged.

"Sure, go ahead," he said, standing and waving an almost perfectly square hand at the chair he'd just vacated. "Be my guest."

Bone settled himself, ran his fingers neatly over the keyboard, and we watched his first question roll itself out in glowing letters on the dark little screen.

HAS THIS INQUIRY ACTIVATED ANY HERETO-FORE INACTIVE PROGRAM?

Greyer opened his mouth to say something but then left it hanging that way without using it because CLAMP had answered, YES.

WHAT IS THE NAME OF THE PROGRAM ACTI-VATED? Bone typed.

CURIOUS DRAGON, said CLAMP.

Bone looked up at Greyer.

"Are you familiar with 'Curious Dragon'?" he asked, but Greyer, whose ordinarily pale face was turning a little pink, just said, "Excuse me," and leaned over Bone's shoulder in order to type out a string of coded gabble which ended in English with, PLEASE FUR-NISH AUTHOR.

AUTHOR NOT AVAILABLE, said CLAMP.

"Very amusing," said Bone.

Greyer straightened, snapped an order to Ashman, paged through the thick manual Ashman handed him, and then leaned over Bone again to type out another, longer string of gibberish which once again ended with, PLEASE FURNISH AUTHOR.

AUTHOR NOT AVAILABLE, repeated CLAMP.

Greyer glared at Bone.

"Do me a favor," he said, "don't say amusing again, all right? Because Curious Dragon's overriding that last code means Curious Dragon knows our whole book, so it's not funny."

"You'll have to forgive him," I interceded helpfully. "He's always had a strange sense of humor."

I might have enlarged on that as it's an interesting subject, but the screen of CLAMP's monitor had suddenly started making a series of funny patterns beginning with spins and sweeps and swirls and ending with a kind of regular snaky weaving before going back to black except for the little blinking cursor.

"That was quite a light show," I said to Bone. "How did you do it?"

"CLAMP did the whole thing all on its very own, Weston," he said, watching the little screen thoughtfully. "I'm only guessing, of course, but I think it was very probably going through some kind of adjustment."

Then the cursor moved neatly across the screen, leaving a short, simple sentence behind.

THOSE LAST QUESTIONS WERE INTELLIGENT.

And then another.

IS THAT YOU, ENOCH BONE?

Bone sat back in his chair and tapped his fingertips together.

"Interesting," he said. "We must be careful, now."

"I'll be goddamned," said Greyer. The pink in his face had now deepened to a really dangerous-looking dark red and things were standing out on his forehead. "Some nervy son of a bitch actually has the brass-bound balls to be talking to us over CLAMP, am I right?"

"We are in contact," said Bone. "And he is considerably worse than nervy, Mr. Greyer. He is highly dangerous."

He thought a moment, then leaned forward and typed out, YES, THIS IS BONE, AND I MUST SAY I AM MOST DISAPPOINTED TO LEARN THOSE SHARKS DID NOT DEVOUR YOU AS WE'D ALL BELIEVED. ARE YOU AT LEAST MUTILATED?

Greyer, clutching the back of Bone's chair, let out a little snort when he read that.

"I'm sorry if I appear to be grossly impolite with this creature, especially while using your machine," Bone said to him over his shoulder, "but ordinary conversational devices are ineffective with a being like the Mandarin; he brushes them aside."

"Oh, no," said Greyer. "That's fine, that's just fine. Give the bastard hell!"

"Is there some way of tracing this communication?"

"Get on it, Ashman," Greyer snapped, watching the Mandarin's reply roll across the screen of what once had been his favorite toy.

IT IS SADDENING TO SEE THAT EVEN GREAT AGE HAS FAILED TO BRING YOU WISDOM, MR. BONE. DESPITE YOUR PAST IMPERTINENCES, I HAD STILL HOPED YOU MIGHT YET GRASP THE GLORY OF MY MISSION, BUT I NOW SEE THIS WAS MERELY AN ANCIENT'S KINDLY DREAMING.

"The old villain's still trying to get you and your brain on his team," I said. "Remember the time he tried to switch you around with that weird drug in the temple at Karnak?"

"I most certainly do," said Bone. "How is the tracing going?"

"It's initiated and in process," said Ashman, looking up from a phone in another corner of the room.

Bone nodded and turned back to the keyboard.

BOSH, he typed. PATHETIC DRIVEL. WHAT HAS YOUR CAREER BEEN, AFTER ALL, BUT A SERIES OF DISMAL HIDING PLACES, A MISERABLE SCUTTLE FROM ONE RAT HOLE TO ANOTHER? HAVE YOU THOUGHT OF GIVING UP AT LAST? PERHAPS IF YOU COOPERATE WITH ME SUFFICIENTLY AN HONORABLE RETIREMENT MIGHT BE ARRANGED.

"Great!" said Greyer, through grinding teeth. "That's the stuff! That'll really get his goat!"

"The trace has gone out to Connecticut," said Ashman.

"It seems somehow unlikely," said Bone.

"Wait a minute," said Ashman. "Now it's snaking back around in this direction."

YOU HAVE GONE TOO FAR, MR. BONE, came the Mandarin's reply. BUT THEN, OF COURSE, YOU ALWAYS DID GO TOO FAR. IT WAS ONE OF YOUR MOST RELIABLE FAILINGS.

"Blast!" said Bone, jerking his hands away from the keyboard. "This thing gave me a nasty shock!"

DID YOU ENJOY THAT, MR. BONE?

"Say, this is really odd," said Ashman, speaking from his corner, "about the trace. It's come all the way back. It's here."

"In the basement," said Bone.

"How did you know?" gasped Ashman.

"He's always in some damned basement," I said.

THIS TIME I SHALL TRIUMPH, BONE! THIS TIME, DOG, I WILL STAND ASTRIDE BOTH YOU AND YOUR SILLY WORLD, AND YOUR RHEUMY EYES' LAST SIGHT WILL BE THE GRINDING OF MY HEEL!

"It's a pity," said Bone, reflectively, "that there is no attachment on this device allowing for diabolical laughter."

But then there was an expanding fireworks display which started with a sudden sputter and spray of sparks traveling back and forth on the edges of CLAMP's gadgets and along its connecting wires, moved right along to roman-candle spews of sparks spraying out from all available corners, and then went on to present a grand finale of explosions, commencing with a variety of small cracking pops and working up to a series of really ear-splitting blasts.

I was just pointing out to Bone that this was probably the diabolical laughter he'd hankered for, when Greyer, who could no longer just stand there and watch all that damage being done to his machine, pushed both Bone and his chair aside and began to type frantically on CLAMP's keyboard.

STOP THIS YOU STOP DOING THIS IF YOU DONT STOP I

But then he went bug-eyed and stiff with his palms flat on the keys and his back arched like a cat's and no matter how hard Ashman and I whacked and shoved him with wooden chairs and thick code books and other nonconducting items, we weren't able to budge him off his beloved CLAMP until the damned thing had thoroughly electrocuted him. Only then did it turn off and let him slump smack across its console.

9

"**D**iabolical laughter, indeed," said Bone, then stole a quiet glance down at the steps of the fancy new escalator on which we were all smoothly descending to the basement of the agency's fancy new building.

"Wondering if the Mandarin's got this thing wired, too?" I asked him out of the corner of my mouth. "I know *I* am."

"I had no idea people built their confounded escalators all the way to their basements," said Bone.

"Don't worry," I said, "I'm sure it'll be the sort of basement that would make any escalator feel right at home. You won't be able to tell it from the sixth floor."

We stood side by side in the center of a formation of agents grouped on the moving stairs, two groups of about a half dozen each, before and behind. They'd taken to forming protective patterns around us because Bone and I had been elevated to expert status since the simultaneous demolition of their boss and CLAMP, and they felt they needed us.

They were all puttering with various gadgets just like Santa's elves, listening to receivers or adjusting knobs, and Ashman, in the lead, was watching the dials and lights of a thing connected to a huge box strapped to the back of an agent by his side, acting as a Sherpa.

Bone looked at all of it with no obvious signs of approval, then gazed inward and sighed.

"You'd think the passing years might at least have slowed him down," he muttered, almost peevishly. "Instead, they only seem to have increased his boldness. But to locate one of his burrows right here in the heart of officialdom does seem rather overdoing it, even for him."

"He's always been a show-off," I said.

I'd guessed right on the basement; it had indirect lighting and no windows and unstainable wall-to-wall carpets, so you couldn't tell the hall from any other hall in the building. Bone and I continued in the passive mode, standing and watching as the agents scuttled busily about with their electronic doohickeys, pressing them to the walls and floors and making them beep and flicker, and eventually they all zeroed in on one particular panel.

"I think this is it," Ashman called out. "We're reading a gap hidden in the ceiling above its top and some kind of trick catch on its bottom."

"Very well," said Bone, as they all looked at him expectantly. "Be sure you stand back from the front of the panel, and work the catch from as far a distance as possible, if you would."

"What do you expect?" asked Ashman. "An explosion? Gas?"

"Nothing that demonstrative," said Bone. "It will be something which would be far less attention-getting, but which would, all the same, quietly and effectively dispose of any solitary person or small group accidently coming across the entrance."

Ashman produced a neat-looking telescopic rod with a sort of robot claw at its end and had been fooling around with the bottom edge of the panel for less than a minute when it suddenly shot up and a nightmare pair of giant steel jaws lunged out and clanged its teeth shut on a corridor-wide chomp of air. Before that had barely registered, the jaws shot back as quick or quicker, and the panel slid neatly shut to hide the damned thing—and, in theory, whatever it might have bit into and taken back to its cave—the instant it whisked back.

"Not bad," said Bone, eyebrows up and lips pursed.

"Very cute," I said. "He hasn't lost his touch. I have to admit that seeing that damn thing takes me back."

"It really does give one rather a nostalgic frisson," admitted Bone. "What do you suppose the capacity of those jaws might be? Three victims? Possibly four?"

"Make it four and parts of five," I said.

Since to the agents this was all brand new, they just mostly stood and gaped.

"Very well," said Bone, after a pause. "Now if you'll trip the panel again, I think you'll find its guardian won't bother you the second time around."

They did, and it shot up a second time, and when nothing happened for long enough the agents crowded in to have a look. Ashman reached up very carefully to touch the point on one of the jaw's double rows of teeth, but he cut his finger on it just the same.

"We've got a horror like this?" he said, staring at us. "Here? In the basement of our own building?"

"That's just for starters," I said. "The Mandarin will have lots more goodies in there. He's very creative, and some of them may even be alive. So let's all stay close together."

People never do listen, so the words were barely out of my mouth when two agents passed by the jaws in order to advance fearlessly down the corridor beyond, which, I observed, followed the usual decor of a Mandarin tunnel by having all its surfaces painted entirely black and restricting its illumination to dim little lights placed at ten-foot intervals in the ceiling.

I have to admit I had a momentary temptation to let them go ahead and be a really unforgettable object lesson for the others—after all, I'm only human. Then the better part of me surfaced and I hurried in after them to head them off, but I'd indulged myself too long and the poor simps were already in trouble.

Sure enough, they hadn't even got near to where the corridor bent to the left and out of sight when a chunk of floor opened up under the first one so slick and neat the second one only just managed to grab hold of his pal's gray flannel jacket, and the two of them set up a caterwauling that was hard to believe.

I snagged them both by their collars like a mother cat and somehow managed to keep them from falling into the pit yawning beneath them until someone got hold of me, and pretty soon everybody managed to get everybody else back to a safe place.

"Okay," I said. "Enough blundering around. Let's have a little orientation session with Mr. Bone."

Bone leaned forward a little on his cane with both hands, kept that pose until all the agents were gathered before him, including the rescued ninnies, and when the sound of gasping and heavy breathing had quieted down to his satisfaction, he opened his eyes, gave them all a thoughtful look, and began to speak.

"Mr. Weston, here, and I have had some small experience with tunnels of the Mandarin, gentlemen, and before we enter this particular structure, it might contribute to our general survival if I passed on some pertinent advice."

He cleared his throat.

"First, as to specifics in your locomotion. One: Make it a routine business before entering any Mandarin tunnel to raise one arm so that the tips of your fingers extend above your head and your forearm protects the side of your neck, thus. Keep it there. Always. In that position the fingers will detect webs or tendrils or claws before they have a chance to attach to your scalp, and the forearm will prevent any successful application of a thuggee strangling noose."

He looked sternly around until he had gathered a few nods.

"Two: Always proceed forward slowly and carefully. I strongly recommend sliding the feet alternately along the ground, keeping the rear foot in place until the front one has traversed something like a yard. This may seem cumbersome, even ludicrous, but it will help alert you to any change in the ground's texture, such as emerging poisoned spikes, or the presence of crawling creatures, or any changing inclination of its surface—as with the trapdoor just experienced by your comrades. Also, if you trip the trigger of some devilish apparatus or nudge some groping creature, the thing may succeed only in grabbing your advanced foot, thus leaving the rest of you free to attack or attempt escape.

"Studiously avoid any areas marked off by painted lines, particularly luminescent ones. A shimmering in the air before you should be probed by the barrel of your gun or some other inanimate object, *never* with your bare hand. Keep your ears peeled for any strange noises, but pay particular attention to what I can fairly describe as a gritty clicking, and if you hear a low, warbling whistle, commence firing even if you see nothing at all. Almost especially if you see nothing at all."

He paused, looked thoughtfully up, then smiled and nodded at the agents.

"I think that will do," he said.

We started off into the tunnel in the escalator formation, half the agents behind us and half before, with Ashman in the lead, everybody following Bone's locomotion specifics which, in no time at all, paid off.

"I think I feel something with my toe!" Ashman called out.

"Well done!" said Bone, smiling. "Let us by, please."

I arrived on his left side and Bone on his right, then Bone had him pull his foot back and probed the black floor ahead of us with his cane.

"What did it feel like, Mr. Ashman?" he asked.

"Like snakes," said Ashman. "Wet. Slimy, I think."

"Ah," said Bone, peering this way and that. "Did you see anything?"

"Only a kind of blur," said Ashman. "Like it whipped back around that corner after I touched it."

"So it's visible, at least," I said.

"Do you have grenades?" Bone asked.

"My God, no," said Ashman, "I never thought of grenades!"

"Get together three of your best shots with your largest guns, I don't think you can use more and hope for unison, and have them lean round that corner and immediately fire as one. They must do this without any attempt to understand or analyze what they're shooting at because if they stop to look at it they may only stand and gape." Bone stepped back. "Tell them to continue firing until whatever it is has stopped moving altogether. Do it now."

Ashman did and the three marksmen did and the noise of the shooting was loud enough to hurt, but we didn't mind in the least when we edged our way around the corner and saw what had been killed.

"I *thought* so," said Bone, almost chuckling, "it's that ghastly land squid he developed in the caverns under Monte Carlo! He's improved on it too, by George. *Look at those mandibles!* And he's got it all black now so it's really hard to see."

"They still die just as messy," I said, then I told the agents to reform the group and move on, and they obeyed their orders, stepping over and through the squid without a murmur. When we came to the first branching of the tunnel, Bone had Ashman fire some good-sized holes into the floor to mark where we'd just come from, and after some discussion as to whether we should turn left or right we chose right because somebody figured we might as well head uptown.

A few branches later Ashman almost got his foot chopped off when a trick guillotine dropped from a slot in the ceiling, so Bone established a regular rotation of the front man in order to spread around the risk and avoid burnout, and a few branches after that we took a break because we had to reload after almost being killed by a half-dozen oversized, armed baboons which had charged out at us from the tunnel ahead. We'd finally managed to wipe them out, but it hadn't been easy because they'd all been dressed in heavy armor which simultaneously bounced bullets and make them look like a bunch of nightmare samurai.

So far that had been it except for the occasional trick dart zipping out from slots in the walls, unidentified somethings that skittered around the floor quickly enough to avoid the agents' frantic stomping, and any number of new trapdoors, including a few really cute ones that waited until you put all your weight on them before they opened underneath your feet.

"Where do you figure we are?" I asked Ashman.

"That's easy," said Ashman. "Somewhere in the seventh circle of hell, right? But up there I'd say we're around Fifth Avenue and Thirty-something Street. Unless we've wandered under Central Park or the East River. I know this thing is here because I'm standing in it, but how did that Mandarin of yours manage to burrow his way through all this Manhattan granite without setting off one hell of a lot of really noticeable explosions?"

"Simple," I said. "He invented the first really effective laser ray back around the end of World War I. The prototype was crude, but if you know where to look there's still a smooth piece missing from the underside of Waterloo Bridge. His present model's only problem would be avoiding city plumbing and the Lexington Avenue subway."

From the look on his face I'm pretty sure Ashman was going to ask another question, but the agent currently taking the lead yelled for someone to come quick so I bustled over. When I got there I saw there'd really been no need to hurry because everything had all happened long ago.

The agent who'd shouted was on one knee and was picking his way through something splotchy-green in his hand which, using a little imagination, I made out had once been someone's wallet. There were three shapes on the ground, now a little less than man-sized, and they were also splotchy-green, but they required a lot less imagination on account of the skulls.

"It's White," the agent said, waving a plastic card he'd pulled from his wallet. "And those have got to be Slate and Blancher beside him. They disappeared two years ago while investigating the Broome Street explosion. We all thought sure Scarlatti's bunch had got them."

"So we weren't the first to find this place," said Ashman.

"I never thought that likely," said Bone. "This maze is like a huge Venus' flytrap. It doubtless has many other entrances for the curious to stumble into, and is probably cluttered with victims. It's not finding the place that counts, but surviving to tell others of your adventures in it. Did we, for example, take the time to leave any report behind before we wandered in?"

"No," said Ashman, losing a little color.

"You see what I mean," Bone said.

Bone studied Ashman studying the bodies, and then the two of us drifted quietly down the corridor a little.

"Blast," Bone hissed, "I could kick myself! That was an inexcusably foolish thing for me to say!"

"I think you spooked him pretty good," I whispered. "Congratulations on terrifying the staff."

"These fellows are brave enough," Bone sighed, "but this discovery may have lent a new reality to their present pickle. With or without my idiotic comments. Do you share my feeling we've moved close?"

"I do," I said. "The trap patterns fit, and he wouldn't throw those costumed monkeys away on an unimportant area. Also, I know for sure those dead agents were dragged here to get them out of the fringes; they'd never have made it this deep on their own. This is definitely inside ground."

"All right, then," said Bone, "let's see if we can persuade our friends to carry on just a little bit farther."

We turned to rejoin them, but there was not a one of them in sight and all was silent except for water dripping in some side tunnel far off enough to work up a good, spooky echo. For a half second I almost believed the agents had snuck off, but then I realized that the corridor had grown two yards shorter and now turned the other way.

"I'm afraid the matter's been taken out of our hands," I said.

10

After making a sincere but completely unsuccessful attempt to figure out how to put the wall back where it had been before it had cut us off from the others, Bone and I decided to head down the tunnel from which the apes had charged us because we suspected the wall had closed down for the specific purpose of sealing that way off from our group.

We moved along in prescribed Mandarin-tunnel style, sliding our feet carefully before us, and keeping our eyes and ears open for various signs and hints the two of us had learned to look for through the years, and while we wished the agents well, it did feel kind of good to be back on our own again.

"Look at that," said Bone, pointing with his cane to a leggy green thing crouching in a niche, "a Cuban tree spider! I haven't seen one of those since that business in the Devon manor."

"I bet I get it dead center on the first shot," I said.

Bone waved his hand airily.

"A waste of ammunition," he said. "I always found the creatures highly overrated."

That didn't stop me from keeping my eye on it as we passed by, and I also gave my full attention to a wall scythe that took some pretty fancy jamming, and then there was a six-foot-high, nasty-looking sort of gray beehive which I sneaked up on and plugged shut with my coat before any of the things I heard buzzing and bumping around inside had a chance to get out.

We came to the first Y-shaped fork—all the others had been Ts—and I was looking back and forth from the one branch to the other, trying to decide which one to take, when it dawned on me that Bone's gaze was glued firmly on the prow of the wall which divided the two of them.

"You have an idea?" I asked.

"More of an instinct," he said. "Prerational."

"Your Japanese philosopher Dogen."

"Just so," he said and, hooking the handle of his cane in the crook of his arm, he reached out and pressed a stone in the wall. His eyes brightened, and he grinned.

"I'm right!" he hissed, pressing another stone, and then another.

"You feel them giving?" I asked.

"I do," he said, "and I know, Weston, in my heart, in my very bones, that the combination is the exact same one he used in that Peking palace."

"The one based on Hexagram Sixty-two of the *I Ching*," I said. " 'The Small Get By.' Why it's his favorite I'll never know."

"That very one," he said, with a grunt and a sigh and various other noises because he was stooping down and pressing the last stone in the series.

Then he straightened and struck a pose of triumph beside me as, with a soft, steady rumble, the corner rose up smoothly into the ceiling and we found ourselves looking through a narrow opening into the start of a corkscrew stone stairway.

"A very pretty little victory," said Bone.

"It is," I said. "You haven't lost the knack."

I took the lead, pointing my gun around the turns, and though all the climbing was pretty hard on Bone and though we had to stop a couple of times for him to recover his breath and get his limbs in order, he never grumbled. About two stories up we reached the entrance to what seemed to be a kind of guardroom with weird, mean-looking weapons in neat rows on racks and a collection of metal halters hanging from chains mounted along one wall.

"It smells like a badly run zoo," I said. "My guess is those apes were quartered here."

"They made it obvious in that encounter they were a good deal more intelligent than your run-of-the-mill simian," said Bone. "I suspected he'd altered their cranial structures, but I wasn't sure because of those helmets."

Next was what seemed to be an elegant sort of waiting room, complete with posh Louis the Something couches any prominent ambassador would be proud to cool his heels on. There was a small door at either side, but we opted for a huge, multipaneled double door straight ahead, and it led us directly into a room which had to be the fulfillment of every world dictator's secret dream. It was the totally successful execution of the kind of high-style bullyboy decor they've all tried to rise to at the peaks of their various Reichs and regimes, but never quite pulled off.

The first thing that caught your eye was an enormous, idealized portrait of the Mandarin hanging over a kind of executive golden throne which squatted regally in back of what had to be the biggest top-management desk ever made to order.

"I kind of miss that full-length statue of himself he had set up in the *Schloss*," I said, after a pause, "but, all in all, I think it's his best effort yet."

"It is hard to believe a man so formidable willingly stoops to such pathetic vulgarity," said Bone. "I shall never understand how an intellect as extraordinary as his is content to play with such toys."

He prodded the dragons in the carpet before him

carefully with his cane as he advanced, and eventually rounded the desk.

"He certainly is a creature of habit," he said. "Ah, this is no doubt the apparatus with which he worked his little games on poor Greyer's CLAMP, and I see he has installed the traditional control panel at the rear of his desk. I'll wager the center button performs its usual function."

"Opens the trap to which the visitor's chair is bolted, and tilts him right into the pit beneath?"

"Exactly. Full of crocodiles."

"Sometimes cobras," I said. "Once even a regular lions' den."

"I'm not even going to bother to try it and find out." Bone blinked and looked at me. "Of course you've noticed."

"Sure," I said. "Everybody's gone. That means we'd better get the hell out of here, and quick, before he blows it all up, or burns it down, or whichever."

"I've been going on the assumption he wouldn't be able to bring himself to destroy it before giving us a chance to look around a bit and admire all its glories," said Bone, "but you're right. We must be careful not to give him the satisfaction of eradicating us along with his latest earthly paradise."

"Do you want to try these two doors behind the desk first, or those out in the waiting room?"

"The ones in here, I think," said Bone. "Since it would be totally out of character for him to reserve a prize exit for his visitors. This one a mere lunge from the desk, perhaps?"

I compared each with the other, but couldn't see much to choose between them; they seemed to be the sort of matched doors you'd expect to come across in any gaudy throne room. I walked over to the door Bone had indicated, pressed my back to the wall beside it, then leaned over and shot my hand out and back quick as a snake opening the thing because, of course, I expected a giant vat of acid or a brace of rockets, but after about a half minute of nothing happening I leaned over and peered in.

"A closet," I said, reaching in and holding out a broad, gold-embroidered sleeve, "containing royal robes."

Bone edged around from its other side, then poked his cane in and pushed over some of the finery to make a little tunnel to the back. There was nothing behind it but a wall.

"Very well," said Bone, "let us try the other one. Do you smell any gas? Any smoke? Any excess ozone?"

"Not yet," I said, and we took our positions around the new door.

"You just flick the knob, this time," said Bone, "and I'll pull it open with my cane."

We did it that way and a good thing, too, because the whole door shot straight out into the air, hinges and all, flew across the room, and smashed against the opposite wall. Then, roaring out from the hole that was left, rolling on spiky treads which chewed up the carpet entirely and raised hell with the parquet underneath, came a small, mean tank topped by a firing rapid-fire cannon mounted on a swivel and backed up by two other smaller cannons firing alternately from its right and left front.

I'll confess that all this to-do, together with its instant total destruction of the opposite wall, struck me as very impressive, but it didn't seem to cut much mustard with Bone because he started to stroll calmly by its side, like someone taking his dog for a quiet walk along a country road, and then, after giving its bottom parts a long, judicious squint, I saw him aim his cane like a sword and, with perfect timing, dart it neatly past some mean-looking gears and thrust it firmly and carefully into the tank tread's works. Then, and only then, did he behave as if he were faced with something more than ordinarily dangerous by hopping aside as quickly as a rabbit ducking a fox.

The tank made a funny, chewing noise which got worse, turned in a sharp lurch to the right, then jammed to a total halt facing the Mandarin's portrait, and proceeded to pulverize that work of art and the wall behind it into a drifting cloud of colorful canvas fragments and gilded wood chips until a brief series of metal hiccups announced it had run out of bullets to waste.

"Really," said Bone. "By now I'd have thought he would have given up on attempts to develop that ridiculous device. Perhaps it's the pet project of some underling."

"I know you never fail to dismantle the damn thing like a kid's toy," I said, "but it always startles the hell out of me, I don't know why. Maybe it's some kind of a phobia. Maybe it's just the noise."

We checked the cubby it had rolled out of, just in case, but it was only a storage bin for spare parts and ammo, so we were halfway toward the outer room when I held up a hand.

"Listen," I said. "Do you hear it?"

Bone leaned forward, tilted his head a little, and squinched up his eyes, producing a cascade of wrinkles on either cheek.

"Yes," he said, "I do. A sort of rushing noise, faint and far away."

That got us moving a little faster on checking out the exits in the waiting room, but they were both a waste of time, each in their own little ways. The one on the left was a dead end because it was a butler's pantry, all stocked and ready to serve magnums of champagne and silver trays of petits fours to kings and suchlike waiting for an audience with the Mandarin, and while the one on the right had once no doubt been a perfectly acceptable hallway, leading gracefully up and out to sunny streets, it was now also a dead end because someone had done careful things to it with explosives so that after a few yards it turned into wall-to-wall and floor-to-ceiling concrete rubble.

"Unfortunate," said Bone, with a sigh. "We may have to grope our way out through the tunnels, after all."

Crossing through the apes' armory, the sound we'd heard only faintly before was now easily identifiable.

"Water," I said. "And lots of it."

I opened the door to the corkscrew stairway, shouted, "*Get back, quick!*" slammed it shut as hard and fast as I could, and started stamping as flat and dead as possible a number of things which had managed to crawl in onto the floor.

"What in heaven's name?" asked Bone.

"I'm grateful I only had a glimpse," I said, leaning hard against the door. "The bastard's flooding the place, all right, and the whole menagerie of monsters he's stocked it with are coming up those stairs like a subway crowd at rush hour!"

Something bumped against the door and something else scratched at it hard, meaning business. Further down two animals were roaring large roars at each other, starting up what sounded like a really serious battle, probably because they were too big to let each other by.

"The steps are covered with crawling things, all sizes," I said. "Bugs, snakes, something that looks like it's all pincers, something else like a big fried egg with an eye in its yolk, and there's a bunch of one kind of thing flapping in the air with stingers, and another bunch like bats, only they're trailing long, red hair."

Bone looked at me.

"I take it that's merely for starters," he said.

"You take it right," I said.

The clawing and digging at the door had increased

steadily along with the squalling and scuffling on the stairs, but it was suddenly all drowned out and silenced by an enormous, echoing howl of rage.

"What could that be?" asked Bone, touching his lips with his fingers, and I saw he'd gone paper-pale.

"All the other things shut up," I whispered. "They're as scared as we are."

Then, even worse than that howl, the two huge roarers began screaming high-pitched screams because, obviously, the howler had started tearing them apart.

Bone and I moved as fast as we could across that armory and there was an awful moment when the door to the waiting room stuck and I thought it might be a trap, but it wasn't and we managed to scuttle and stumble our way back to the throne room and we shut and locked every door behind us and piled heavy heaps of stuff in front of every one of them.

We did our best to keep calm—ordinarily we're pretty good at it—trying to find secret panels in the wall, traps in the floor or ceiling, any way out, but we heard the door from the corkscrew stairway crash open, and then we heard the door leading to the waiting room crash open after that, and just as something with huge things to do it with started pounding on the big double door to the throne room and making it bulge in with each pounding, we saw water working its way through the crack under the door and over the dragons on the carpet, starting as a seep and building quickly to a smooth pouring.

First we looked at each other, second we looked once again around the walls, and then Bone made a fist and banged it into the palm of his other hand.

"The clothes closet!" he said.

"I suppose it'll give us a minute," I said.

"No, no—that's not what I mean, Weston!" he snapped. "Check the back of it! Behind those silly regal robes!"

I did, as quickly and as skillfully as I knew how, and he was right as usual and the rear wall of it slid to one side just as sweet as you could wish for.

"It's an elevator," I shouted. "It's a goddamn elevator!"

At once Bone was crowded in it beside me and I was pushing the top button—there were just two buttons, UP and DOWN—just as we heard the door to the throne room cave in, and the elevator only barely managed to get started up when its outside doors were pounded in hard enough to bang them against the bottom of the cage and knock it a little sidewise, but that didn't stop the elevator from going up after an initial falter and a little noisy grating against the back of the shaft, and after that it rose slick and fast because the thing down there didn't have the brains to grab at its cables, which we were both afraid it would do, though I will admit it did seem to take a long, long time before we got high enough for its howls to fade away.

11

The elevator doors opened, with an *Alice in Wonderland* kind of logic, on another closet, although a much more conventional one, containing tweeds and soft felt hats instead of golden robes and crowns. We stepped out into it and the elevator closed behind us and was in turn covered by the silent slide down of a paneled oak wall which matched the others in the little room.

I felt Bone stiffen beside me and turned to see him frowning at a suitcase, a nice old alligator-hide number.

"Good heavens!" he said. "Look at that! It's incredible!"

"That description might be a little strong," I said, but I looked it over since he'd asked me and failed to find anything particularly incredible about it until I spotted the faded gold initials stamped on a flat bit of leather sewn near its handle: E. B.

"Is it possible?" I asked.

"That is my suitcase!" said Bone, and then he straightened and pointed at the shelves and hangers. "These are my clothes!" He stepped forward, opened the closet door, and waved at the space beyond. "This is my bedroom!"

I followed, did a quick look around, then headed for the floor-to-ceiling windows for a long, slow gape at what turned out to be the glories of Park Avenue below.

"We're in the confounded Presidential Suite!" roared Bone, and he doesn't often roar so it means something when he does. "I could have been slaughtered in my sleep any time that mad villain took the whim! Those agency people are fools! I've been drafted by total incompetents!"

He didn't exactly stride—at his age it just isn't possible—but he came close to it, crossing the floor of the bedroom. He'd thrown open the door to the big living room and had started to continue his near-stride across that, probably with the idea of near-striding entirely the hell out of the Barton Towers and away forever, when he suddenly brought himself up short, as did I, because seven men wearing dark glasses and three-piece suits of varying shades of gray were very firmly and skillfully pointing large guns at us.

"That may be your bedroom," I said to Bone, "but I think this has stopped being your living room."

"Down on the floor," said one of the men.

"Spread out," said another.

I was all for cooperating, and had even got started, but Bone, standing as straight as he was able, and distributing his glare evenly on all concerned, said, "Never."

This seemed to have a bad effect on the three-piecers, but what they would have done about it, if left on their own, will have to remain a mystery forever because at that exact moment the outer door was opened by one of the marines they kept there for that purpose and a hearty-looking man wearing a much better tailored gray suit than any other present breezed in with a great air of authority and a lot of instructions.

"Boys, boys—put up your guns at once!" he said, waving his big, pink hands as he issued orders. "Good grief, don't you know that's Enoch Bone? Okay, now, you all leave us alone and keep on tidying up. You, Silverman, get on the phone in some other room to One and tell them to keep flying him around up there in the air where it's safe; we don't want him waiting in the lobby. Mr. Bone, Mr. Weston, please accept my apologies; I see our ID photos on you are really out of date! Do let's sit down by the window, here, and catch up. My name is Hewliss, Ben Hewliss, I head up the agency; do my best, but things like this just happen."

Bone settled in a chair, after a significant pause, but I remained standing in back of him in a kind of guardian position. It had been proper etiquette for Ben Hewliss to introduce himself, but it borders on false modesty when a national monument acts as though you need to learn his name. Hewliss had been running his agency, everybody thought of it as his, through six different administrations, and he'd been a powerful factor in every one of them. He was a large, rumpled man with a big, skillful smile stretching from one side to the other of his wide, open-seeming face, and I never could figure out if he couldn't quite hide the foxiness in his eyes, or if he let it show on purpose.

"I don't mind saying you boys have given us some pretty fancy worrying," said Hewliss, leaning close to Bone and then smoothly leaning back when he saw Bone didn't like it. "The whole bunch of you just vanishing, and Greyer dead; good grief, it had us climbing walls! Then Ashman calls in five minutes ago—he'll be here as soon as he can make it; they relayed him to me in the car coming over—and tells me how he and his bunch surfaced in a tunnel in Central Park, the one next to the merry-go-round; tells me how they just missed drowning like rats and how the whole damn area's near to flooded with the water that came out after them; said as how you boys were probably dead and gone in that awful place, but, good grief, here you are! It's wonderful! How'd you ever do it? And turn up here? How did you ever manage to turn up here, Mr. Bone?"

Bone told him and though Hewliss didn't get any less folksy, the story turned him from a friendly farmer type to the tough, backwoods sheriff variety in pretty quick order, especially the part about the elevator.

"Silverman?" He'd pulled out and unfolded a pocket intercom and was talking into it. "Get some frogmen here on the double, on the triple, the best, and they may have to do some fancy climbing, and they'll for damn sure have to do some fancy blowing up. And fly those trick-wall experts in pronto. How'd he take it up there on One? Good. Maybe he can have a little snack. Let them know we're shifting him to the other bedroom in the suite just for the afternoon. I know he won't like it, but it has to be done."

He snapped his gadget shut and studied us.

"We'll cork that shaft you boys came up in, and we'll cork it good," he said, and shook his head. "It's a mercy you found it, boys, it's a proper mercy. I've got reports on what you've said of these folks, Mr. Bone, about these devil people you're stirred up about, the China-man, the Frenchman, and the Limey, and I had my doubts as to them being behind that awful business in D.C., but no longer, sir. I am now convinced those are the villains. My blood runs cold when I think what might have happened if you and Mr. Weston, here, hadn't wrecked their game. Say, you boys are up for medals on this, don't think you aren't. The president might have been killed! In there! This very night!"

"The One you keep mentioning is then Air Force One," said Bone.

"Right," said Hewliss, nodding. "President Parker will be arriving when we get things in place. Mrs. Parker was all set to come with him, only when the boys were clearing out those secret walls they uncovered some of the original wallpaper in two of the halls and she's had it copied and is mad to put it up. I can tell you that woman's worked wonders with the old homestead!"

"You can't be serious," said Bone. "You're going to let him stay here? In this suite? After what Weston and I discovered?"

Hewitt leaned forward and then quickly leaned back because he remembered Bone hadn't liked it the first time.

"But you scotched it, Mr. Bone," he said, bringing back the smile. "You stopped them cold. They had a direct connection, but it's gone because of you. Look, you heard me asking for the secret-panel experts—you hear everything—the president won't sleep here until it's all been checked to a fare-thee-well. Another thing, Mr. Bone, it's important to grasp this, the president just loves stopping at the Presidential Suite of the Barton Towers, especially while being the president, you understand? It makes it all kind of official for him. Do you follow me on this?"

"You have explained yourself properly, at last, Mr. Hewliss," said Bone, standing. "You are both guardian and courtier, and the duties overlap. I see your men filing out of both Mr. Weston's bedroom and mine with our belongings. We are, of course, to be lodged elsewhere."

"The suite directly below this one, sir." Hewliss rose and we started for the door. "It's practically a duplicate."

"But not quite as good," said Bone. "Otherwise, what's the point of being president?"

The door was marine-opened and Hewliss led us to the elevator at the far end of the bank.

"It's for staff only," he said, as we glided down. "Services just this floor and the one beneath it. The two floors together make up the high-security area. Perhaps you'd like to have a look-see at our command area before you get settled? It's right next door to your new quarters. We want you handy to the action, sir."

"Very well," said Bone, and we were led into a ceiling-lit, high-tech security paradise which was a look-alike extension of the agency's downtown digs except that here they seemed to go in more for tv monitors. One wall was entirely covered with them, and they were all on, every damned one of them.

"It makes me ill to look at all those miserable, ugly little pictures," said Bone.

"You need the knack, I'll hand you that," said Hewliss. "Helps if you sort of let your eye rove and not get fixed on any one image. Right now over here's the coverage of the suite upstairs, not much going on except agents vacuuming and dusting. You've probably noticed we didn't think to put a camera in that damned closet with the elevator you boys discovered, but we'll take care of that. Here's the hall and I see the frogmen have turned up, and, yes, by golly, there's Ashman with them."

He unfolded his little pocket intercom.

"Ashman?" he said, and Ashman's tiny images, three of them seen from three points of view, looked up and listened. "Hewliss, here. Good to see you. Bone and Weston are with me in Command and both okay; tell you about it later. What's up?"

"I was really happy to hear you two made it, Mr. Bone, Mr. Weston," Ashman said in tinny stereo from some overhead speakers. "I'm going with the frogmen, sir. I want to have a look at the other end of that place."

"Go to it. Over and out," Hewliss said, folding up his intercom and continuing his little guided tour of the television screens. "Then, Mr. Bone, Mr. Weston, here's the hotel entrance, lobby, elevator up, all that. And over here we've got the left bank of monitors on Air Force One, the president's plane. Interior stuff here, executive cabins, pilot's cabin, and so on, and exterior views here, from all those places."

"What is that?" asked Bone, pointing.

The little read-out underneath identified the image on the screen Bone had singled out as being the view from the left of the central executive cabin. It showed sky, clouds, and a funny little violet-colored blotch on the lower-right corner. The blotch seemed to be coming closer, and Hewliss leaned over and tapped the shoulder of a man wearing an earphone and trying to keep track of a control panel packed with dials and screens.

"How about the radar?" Hewliss asked him.

"Nothing, sir," the man said, and yet the blotch had become bigger.

"You have a way of coming across things, Mr. Bone," said Hewliss, "I swear you do." He flipped open his intercom and tapped out some code on its pad. "Pilot One? This is Hewliss. Do you read me? Over."

"Yessir," said the pilot, tinny, like Ashman, but mono. "Over."

"You see that thing? To port? Around nine o'clock? Over."

There was a pause during which we heard the sounds of the plane's engines and various clicks and clatters from the pilot's cabin, and then, "Yessir. Only it doesn't quite look real, sir. It's like I had something in my eye. And I'm not picking it up on radar. Maybe it's an illusion. Over."

"Yeah, well, we're having the same illusion down here," said Hewliss. "Fly away from it and see what happens. Over." He tapped the shoulder of the man on the table. "Bring that thing up on a couple of other screens," he told him. "Bring it about three times up on one and fill the screen with it on the other."

He did, but all that happened was that you saw a bigger violet blotch. It changed its position as our point of view altered from the pilot's turning.

"Look," said Hewliss, "it's getting smaller as he pulls away. So it's really there; it's a something."

"Do you have weapons on that plane?" asked Bone.

"No," said Hewliss. "Better. It's escorted." He spoke to the pilot. "Bring in the fighters," he told him, "with instructions to destroy that thing. And you continue getting the hell out of there. Over."

There was a spate of aeronautical-type gobbledegook back and forth from the speakers, and two jet fighters glistened into view. They began shrinking at once because Air Force One was leaving the vicinity as quickly as possible, but we saw them swooping down and throwing a lot of fire at the splotch with no particular effect. Hewliss leaned down over the man at the table.

"You got a kind of telescope at the rear," he said. "Train in on all that. Bring it up before we lose our fix on those planes."

The man's hand flickered over his controls and two of the monitors started showing long-distance shots of the fighters still figure-eighting in on the splotch, still not seeming to be able to do it any damage.

"If those boys can just keep that damn thing busy," said Hewliss, "I'll settle for that."

Then there was a bright flash and we had only a brief glimpse more before the angle changed hopelessly and we lost view of the fight altogether, but that was enough to show us that while one of the planes was still going hell for leather after the splotch, the other one was just gone with no trace at all.

"Mr. Hewliss, sir," came the pilot's voice over the intercom. "We're landing. We'll be safe on the ground in a moment. And I think we're damned lucky to have made it. Over."

Hewliss sighed and leaned hard on the chair back of the man at the table.

"You got that right," he said.

12

With five restaurants in the Barton, you'd think they'd have managed to make at least one of them good, but the only impressive thing about their main room, La Salle d'Or, is the total on the check they hand you after you've worked your way through the meal. I'd wanted to take Athenee to a better place for lunch, since it had been so many years since our last one, and since she knows the difference between a good meal and what they serve at La Salle d'Or, but the president was going to see Bone and me "sometime" that afternoon, so I was staying in the building in order to be within a lackey's dash of his suite.

"Bone says the flying violet blotch has got to be a production of the Professor," I said, leaning back as the waiter removed my hors d'oeuvre dishes and cutlery from the wrong side. "He says the Mandarin's a brilliant scientist, all right, but his expertise leans to what Bone calls the 'fiendish biological,' whereas this thing appears to be high physics. And your father, while no slouch at whipping up cute murder weapons and nifty burglar tools, is only a clever handyman compared to those other two."

"He is right," said Athenee. "Papa is no scientist, and, outside of breeding those winged monsters of his, the Mandarin has never been all that clever with flying things. Of course there was that ribbed cape with which he glided off the tip of a skyscraper when the police thought they had him cornered; but then his mechanical pterodactyl was a complete disaster."

The captain brought the entree then and I suppose I should tell you I recall clearly what it was since I'm supposed to be better than average at noticing things and filing them away, but the truth is the only thing I really remember about that lunch is how Athenee looked; how her jaws moved when she chewed, how her throat rippled when she swallowed, and I could recite you word for word everything she said.

A lot of it was brand new to me; for example, the fact that her father had taught her early how to steal, the same as you start to teach a ballet dancer when it's still a little kid.

"He began by having me sneak around his study while he worked, to see if I could find a bonbon which he'd concealed somewhere inside the room," she told me. "If I could locate it without his hearing me it was mine, but if he caught me making the slightest sound he would take the candy from its hiding place and drop it into a large tank of piranha which he kept by his desk. They particularly loved chocolate-covered coconut.

"Of course I learned a lot from the books on thievery in his library, and more from working with the collection of safes and man traps in his workshop, but the heart of his teaching was practical experience. He would, for instance, put me outside the walls of the estate at dusk and if I wanted dinner—which, being a growing child, I most certainly did—I had to make my way back in, entirely unobserved despite the many locks and alarms, ancient and modern, which he changed daily for my benefit."

"Kind of tough," I said.

"It was, in its way, lovingly done. By the age of thirteen I was by far the most accomplished cat burglar operating on the Cote d'Azur. Of course it was all marvelously entertaining; it was far better than hopscotch and tag and hide-and-seek all rolled into one.

"I had the most charming black tights you could imagine; a pretty, silver-plated set of picks and jimmies; and a lovely cape with a hood and a special pouch to hold the loot. I could climb any wall, was soundless on the most fragile roof tiles, and was able to squeeze through openings which would have defeated the most agile full-grown second-story thief."

"Were you ever caught?" I asked her.

"Once," she said. "It was in an exquisite château, perfect of its kind, and beautifully furnished. I had made my way easily to the inner chamber that was my goal when the beam of my flashlight played across a gorgeous Gobelin tapestry showing rabbits and birds playing in a bower of flowers. I stood entranced at the sight and did not hear the countess coming up behind me.

"She held a golden, jeweled pistol, very small but very serious, and she pointed it expertly at my heart. She had caught me in her treasure chamber, the very fulcrum of her power, and there was no mercy in her eyes. Make no mistake, she could and would have killed me then and there but for my stratagem."

"What was your stratagem?" I asked.

"I wept," Athenee said. "I wept like a frightened little girl would do until the countess relented and lowered her gun and patted my head. She was a lovely lady, somewhere in her nineties, and very fragile, but I knew she was very tough and probably only used that fragility as another weapon, as I had used my tears.

"She fed me crunchy little cookies which came from my favorite shop in Nice, and a potful of cocoa to wash them down, and the two of us talked all night long. I told her more than I had ever told anyone in my life, enough to guillotine my father many times over I'm sure. She consoled me for my loneliness and held me close and told me secrets, too: how sad she was that she'd given a child away in her youth, and how pleased she was that she'd poisoned the late count at last and nobody had ever found her out.

"When the dim light that comes just before dawn showed the edges of the trees in the château's garden below she gave me the tiara my father had sent me to steal, saying it had come from a wicked family after all and she was glad to be rid of it, and besides, it was fully insured. Then she kissed me on the forehead and called me by a baby name that I think meant a good deal to her, and I left."

By the time dessert was finished and we were stirring our second cups of coffee, Athenee and I had worked our way through a number of things that needed going into and, once we'd done all right with those, we admitted that we'd missed one another pretty badly and that we believed we might work things out after all, given half a chance, and that led, naturally enough, to my reaching out and taking her hand.

"I wondered if you were ever going to do that," she said.

"So did I," I said, "but not much."

"Why did you waste all that time being Mr. Bowen in Elmsville, John?" she asked.

"I grew up in a town like that," I said. "Even in a house like that. I guess I figured I'd started peacefully and maybe I could end peacefully. Probably it was silly."

"And then that Mr. Ashman turned up and spoiled it all for you," she said.

"But here we are together again," I said. "So maybe Ashman's not so bad, after all."

"One should never speak of the devil," said Athenee, and I turned around at a touch of my shoulder to see Ashman looking down at us.

"Sorry to disturb you," he said. "Particularly because

you look like you're enjoying yourselves. The president's ready to see you and Bone, Weston."

Before we separated, Athenee and I worked out a time and place to continue our conversation that evening if my country didn't need me all that much, and as Ashman spirited me away from her he ran over how his exploration and elevator-cementing expedition had gone.

"There were things down there I don't want to think about," he said. "Particularly the creature we found that had forced itself partway up the shaft, the one you only just got away from. It's the first time I've ever seen anything with a mouth that ran all the way from its nose to its stomach."

"Were there any surviors at all?"

"None we've found so far, but we won't stop the search until we're absolutely sure, take my word for it. This city's tough enough without refugees from those tunnels roaming the streets."

Whatever their other faults, the agency's timing on this maneuver was perfect, as Bone was coming down the hall just as Ashman and I emerged on the top floor, so when the door to the Presidential Suite was opened, by three marines this time, we all made our entrance together.

Hewliss and President Parker had been seated head-to-head at the big coffee table but when they saw us the two of them rose smiling, just as smooth and slick as I'd seen them doing it on tv at dozens of photo opportunities.

"We really appreciate your taking care of this problem, Mr. Bone," said the president, after Hewliss had performed the introductions. "Ben's told me how you foiled that hidden elevator plot, and of the important difference your spotting that flying saucer made, and I'm happy to say he's assured me that with your help we'll track down the evil men responsible in no time at all."

Bone threw a sidewise glance at Hewliss that was not exactly overloaded with gratitude, then returned to gazing respectfully up at Parker.

"I am honored by your confidence in me, Mr. President," he said, "but concerned by the extent of your optimism. All Mr. Weston and I have done so far is to force the Mandarin to abandon an elaborate lair, and to deprive Spectrobert of a highly successful restaurant; but these evil men, as you so aptly described them, including the Professor—who, so far as I know, we have not even inconvenienced—are still very much beyond our reach, sir, and remain a grave, continuing danger to yourself."

"Ah, but you've got them on the run," said Parker, putting a large, friendly hand on Bone's shoulder and never even noticing how skillfully Bone covered his wince. "With you at their heels, these fiends won't be doing much more than trying to cover up their trail. They'll be out of action."

"They are as accustomed to being pursued as I am to pursuing, Mr. President," said Bone. "It is a regular condition with them. Regretfully, I can promise you it won't reduce their scheming."

Parker studied Bone for a minute, shifted his large jaw in thought, then removed his hand and shrugged.

"I guess you're the one who should tell Mr. Bone, here, about the purpose of my visit, Ben," said Parker to Hewliss. "I think he'll probably take it better from a fellow professional."

Hewliss looked at the president, then at Bone, then cleared his throat.

"Well, sure enough. I guess that makes sense," said Hewliss, working his mouth over which words to start with. "You see, Mr. Bone, the thing is, there seems to be a little bit of overlap in your investigation and what the president's come here to do. Nothing serious, understand, but something that might give you concern, so we wanted to be the ones to tell you about it, because, do believe me, it is very important to us, important to the president himself, that you stay on in this business, and fully active, as there are very few people in law enforcement who are as capable as you, or as well informed about these terrible people—hell, most of 'em never even heard of the bastards—and I know your preliminary findings have made some connections between Waldo World and them and all this business—tentative, though, we understand those connections are strictly tentative—so we wanted you to learn from us, personally, that the president intends to visit the place, Waldo World, that is, to commemorate the activation of the President Parker Waldobot since he feels, rightly, I think, that the creation of the thing's a real honor and that the American people have a right to see the actual president standing there when it's turned on. We didn't want you to pick all this up from just anyone."

There was a little silence during which both President Parker and Hewliss shifted but Bone remained perfectly still, and then he broke the silence by moving absolutely nothing but his mouth.

"If I had not committed myself irrevocably to this project, I would now withdraw from the affair," Bone said. "Unfortunately for me, I am bound to it."

He studied the fancy ceiling, trying to find a little calmness up there I guess, rubbed some wrinkles on his forehead at random, tugged at a wattle, and transferred his gaze to the president.

"I assume from Mr. Hewliss's remarks, since he would not have made them otherwise, that you are determined beyond any possible argument on this expedition to Waldo World, Mr. President," he said. "But permit me to say that the connections we've uncovered between that place and these evil men—I employ your apt term again—are not as ephemeral as Mr. Hewliss posits, but solid enough to give me the sincerest apprehension as to your safety, sir, during such an adventure."

The president smiled and raised his hand as if about to touch Bone's shoulder again, but some sixth sense must have warned him that that might have really been too much, so he took hold of his own lapel with it instead, like a statue of Lincoln in a park, and spoke, like a statue of Lincoln in a park would speak if it could.

"I'm afraid that sort of thing goes with the territory, Mr. Bone," he said, putting on a brave but humble expression. "You can't be president these days and not expect some risk during any public appearance. So far I've managed to sidestep the really serious bullets, and, with the help of good people like yourself, my luck may continue to hold."

Bone linked the fingers of his hands together in his lap, which is next to the worst sign there is, but I was relieved to see the thumb tips were pressed together. It's when the fingers are linked and the thumb tips are tapping that you know you've got where Bone calls "beyond the pale."

"Do not make the mistake of confusing these creatures with the befuddled loonies who ordinarily commit assassinations, sir," he said. "Besides, the deeper I go into this business, the more I have increasing doubts that their objective, so far as you are concerned, is assassination at all. I think they wish you worse than sudden death, Mr. President."

I noticed Hewliss look up at him with considerable interest at that, to almost ask a question, and then decide to let it go for now. Bone waited all that out and continued.

"Let me describe to you some of the spectacular cruelties which have set these men apart from the common run of villains, sir, in hopes I can alert you to the depth and ingenuity of their malice and perhaps dissuade you from this reckless visit.

"The Mandarin, for example, in the process of developing a deadly fungus with which he intended to destroy an entire African tribe whose leaders had balked at his orders, tested it out by scattering it on the grounds of an isolated Swiss orphanage. Unfortunately for the children, the spores did not kill them but only softened their bodies, including their bones, and the survivors are rolled about to this day like mollusks in wheeled shells since the mold has the unfortunate side effect of indefinitely extending the lives of those it deforms. The Mandarin thought the progress of the infection too delicate for its intended audience and lacking in dramatic effect, so he disposed of the tribe more sensationally by means of pouring lava over them from an artificially contrived volcano.

"The second of this diabolic trio, the Professor, once developed a sonic device which had the peculiar virtue of being able to incinerate living flesh without in any way affecting inanimate objects. The drawback of his invention was that it could be only crudely localized—small things like banks were too confined for its powers—so the Professor burnt the entire population of a wealthy Bavarian village without damaging any of their township's valuables, and then had his minions loot the entire place, including every last pocket and purse of its smoking inhabitants. On his second try, in Alsace, his men were reduced to chunky ash along with their intended victims and he abandoned further use of the apparatus, though the instant incineration of a famed savings institution in Zurich some years ago leads me to suspect he's still tinkering with it.

"The third member of the group, Spectrobert, is perhaps technically less sophisticated than his vile partners, but he may be the wickedest of the lot. An instructive frolic of his, and I give it this latter description because it totally lacks any motivation save pure viciousness, took place in France between more serious engagements. He descended quietly on one of those small traveling circuses as it was playing its family matinee for a hamlet of Provence one summer afternoon, and while part of his fearsome armed gang surrounded its exterior and covered all its exits, he and the rest of his apaches stole into the tent, took up a position in the center of the tiny circus's one ring during the entrance of the parade of clowns, and, at a signal from Spectrobert, who was wearing a particularly gaudy ringmaster's suit along with his usual black mask, the place was flooded with a simple gas composed of a compound of fierce irritants laced with a leisurely but deadly poison. For the next half hour Spectrobert and his band of rogues—who had all previously swallowed a substance which protected them from the gas's effect—enjoyed the sight of what the poor townsfolk did to one another as panic and the increasing agonies produced by the poison vapors turned them slowly into maniacs mercilessly clawing at their neighbors and relatives in furious and futile attempts at escape. In the end, most of his victims killed one another, just as he had hoped, and almost none of them survived to die of the gas.

"It is a great misfortune for the human race that these three singular monsters, who have heretofore always stalked their prey alone, should have joined forces. The idea that their diverse, sinister abilities and mad ambitions are combined is appalling, particularly so far as you are concerned, Mr. President, since you appear to be the specific target of this ghastly assemblage. Even if the connection between these beings and this absurd Waldo World were as tenuous as Mr. Hewliss maintains it is, and I assure you it is not, it would be folly for you to chance walking into their maw. I beg you to abandon this project!"

President Pat Parker produced a thoughtful expression, held it for a brief moment, and then replaced it with a look of steely determination.

"Mr. Bone," he said, "I won't pretend I'm not moved by what you've just told me about these dreadful people, but I've given my word to Art Waldo that I'd come and visit him, and he's counting on that, and I don't break my word. Hand me that box, Hewliss."

Hewliss reached under the table and passed a basketball-sized box to the president, who rested it on his lap.

"I don't like to make speeches," Parker said, with a perfectly straight face, "but Art Waldo is an important kind of person, not just to the kids—although it matters that a lot of them will grow up better citizens because of his cartoons—but to all of us, because he's a living, breathing symbol of what this great country's about. If going to visit Art's wonderful family-entertainment center because he wants to honor me is taking a chance, well, I'm proud to do it. That's what being the president's all about. But, Mr. Bone, that's not all this visit is about!"

He began opening the box in his lap.

"This trip doesn't just concern a public appearance, Mr. Bone," he said, reaching into the box and taking hold of something resting inside of it, just out of sight. "If it were just that I'm sure that Art, once he knew about the possible dangers, would be the first to say, 'Stay away, Mr. President, stay away!' No, this trip concerns something which may improve not only the conditions of my watch in the office of chief executive of these United States, but that of every other president to follow in my path."

Smiling earnestly, Parker slowly lifted the contents of the box into full view. It was, with its matching smile, a perfect duplicate of his head, except the hair was a little mussed. Bone's thumb tips began tapping.

"If I brave this present danger, Mr. Bone," said Parker, "there is no way of estimating how many future dangers I, and other leading public figures after me, can avoid, because this device, or rather the complete one which Art Waldo is going to show me, is so incredibly more advanced than any of the previous presidential models that it has become far more than a simple device to provide entertainment. It may be the key, for me, to a whole new way of life."

He leaned over to make some adjustments to the head which made it frown and wink one eye and then he looked back up at us, smiling proudly.

"Say, what do you think of that?" he said.

"As you say," muttered Bone, "incredible."

"Marvelous, isn't it?" said the president. "Imagine the dangers which will easily be averted by the simple substitution of one of these machines for me in a motor parade, for example, or the opening of an airport or a bridge. Why, I'm assured it will even be able to deliver minor speeches! And that's not all, Mr. Bone, that's not all. Do you know how much valuable time I waste because I have to greet unimportant delegations each and every week? Not just obscure third-world potentates—I can accept that, I can even see its necessity—but groups of children and old people and pet lovers and I don't know what all with their scrolls and trophies and funny little models somebody's built in their basement and that fall apart when they hand them to me in front of all those cameras. Do you know how many Indian bonnets I have to pose in? How many times I have to stand there shaking hands with everybody in the room?"

He fooled with the head again, bringing back its smile and opening its eye, then he jiggled it on his knee, looking at it the way a father looks at his favorite baby.

"The things I'll be able to get done, Mr. Bone," he said, sighing deeply. "The peace I'll have."

Bone nodded grimly, stood, gave a tight little bow, and since I had made it my business to be right by his side, we walked slowly out of the room together, leaving the president with his heads.

13

I won't take complete credit for getting Bone out of there before something unfortunate happened. I'm sure there was a lot of luck involved or I couldn't have done it at all, but it did take considerable skill nevertheless.

"I know you'd rather I didn't," I said, guiding him carefully down the center of the hallway so he wouldn't get close enough to a wall to start banging on it and injure himself, "but I really have to congratulate you on keeping your trap shut back there. I couldn't even hear your teeth grinding until we cleared the doorway."

"Shut up," he said.

Ashman had hurried out after we'd left and he joined us just as we entered the special elevator. He looked pale and a little confused.

"What do you think," he said as we were lowered to the other floor of the special section, "is the president crazy, or what?"

"I think most sane people probably stopped running for office a while back," I said, keeping my protective hold on Bone while we made our way into the apartment that had been set aside for the two of us, and Ashman followed.

"Okay," I said to Bone, with my arm still around him. "Here we are, all safe and sound. If I let you go now will you promise not to start kicking things?"

He didn't bother to give me an answer, just pulled his

way loose and over to a chair by the window and sat. I watched him take a few deep breaths and reassemble his parts before I said, "So what do you want to do about it all?"

"I've read the folder on that awful place," he said almost calmly, tugging at a dewlap. "I've even memorized the map, as per the inked-in instructions. I understand there's some ghastly hostelry on the premises."

"There is," I said. "They claim it's the motel of the future."

Bone shuddered.

"I'm sure their pessimism is fully justified," he said, then looked up at Ashman. "I assume the president is going to take this idiotic risk almost immediately?"

"The day after tomorrow," Ashman said. "With no announcement. It's to be a surprise visit so far as the public is concerned. And, of course, we'd like to think it'll be a surprise to these other people, though there doesn't seem to be much of a chance of that."

"Very well," Bone said. "Let us establish ourselves there tomorrow morning. We'll leave here at 7:00 A.M. I'd appreciate it if you'd make the arrangements. I have absolutely no plan as to how we'll proceed, but perhaps something will come to me if I sleep on it. Now go away, please."

Athenee and I had a dinner at a respectable restaurant which was almost good enough to make up for lunch, and during the meal and for quite a while after we continued on with ironing out the personal stuff we'd started before, including repair work on some serious mistakes we'd both made which I don't see any point in going into, and that naturally worked us around to making a couple of pretty serious promises, and only after we'd done all that and exchanged a number of longish looks and touches to show we'd meant the promises did we start on business.

My first reaction when she offered to come along was

to get protective and insist she stay away, but the more she went on about how she probably knew her father's modus operandi better than any other human on earth, and how she would have the edge on everybody else in spotting him in whatever disguise he'd cooked up for the occasion, the more I began to figure the protective mode was pretty much out of date and had probably never applied to Athenee in the first place, so by the time we realized we were keeping the restaurant open it had been decided she'd turn up in the morning and come along with us.

I expected a little resistance from Bone when I sprung it on him in the elevator going down—I'd saved it for the last moment because I didn't want to give him a chance to build up a head of steam—but he didn't give me any fight at all.

"I assume you have her waiting in that infernal limousine?" he said, and when I admitted I did he nodded. "She is a clever woman and I have often thought it fortunate for humanity at large that she balked at taking up her father's ways. By all means let her join us. I would even consider any plans she has to offer; Morpheus's inspirations to me last night were rather sketchy, save for a sensible notion to traverse the exact path of the presidential expedition, employing the precise transportation planned. I'm sure it will be quite an ordeal."

But she had no suggestions and neither did Ashman, who was also waiting in the limo, though of course his agency had set in motion the usual security routines which we all assumed would not be sufficient, considering the opposition.

Bone got settled in a window seat, taking his usual firm grip on the strap, then just sat and stared blankly into space, ignoring vision and things like that in order to find out what his waking mind could do with the problem. He kept that up without a break until we emerged from the clump of toll booths on the other side of the river and came within full sight of the statue of Quacky the Duck, which was, I have to admit it, a moment I'd really been waiting for.

"Good heavens," he said, after a moment of silent glaring, "it's far worse than I thought."

"Really something, isn't it?" I said. "Notice how it seems to be waving its wing just at you, personally, like it says in the folder?"

"Rubbish," said Bone.

"Well, I guess a thing like that is always a subjective call," I said. "They say if you spread out Quacky's coat it would cover two football fields, and that the beak could hold a four-door family car, which, of course, could then hold a family. Pretty soon we'll be close enough for you to hear it singing the 'Lucky Duck' song."

We were driven in through a special side road which I hadn't seen before, and at first I figured it was because Waldo World rated a group trying to save the life of the president of the United States even higher than a reporter from *Folks' Magazine*, but when we pulled up in front of the main entrance to Elf Castle and I saw Art Waldo himself pacing back and forth at the foot of the big white stairway in front of the building with his public-relations man Frank Nealy reduced to a mere background figure, I began to suspect there might be some other motivation, and when I got a close look at the eager expression on Waldo's face, I knew what it was. So, as a bunch of small people in elf suits were having trouble opening the doors of our limo because Waldo kept getting in their way trying to peer inside of the passenger compartment, I leaned toward Bone and passed him my deduction from the corner of my mouth.

"Waldo wants something from you," I said. "Something special. I can tell it."

"What?" asked Bone.

"I don't know," I said. "But he wants it very, very

much. He can't wait to ask. Look at the way his hands keep sort of clutching in your direction."

I stepped out before Bone, both to give him strategic little tugs because getting out of limos isn't easy at any age but gets harder as you get older, and to fend off Waldo's pawing which I anticipated and which came.

"Mr. Bone?" said Waldo, speaking eagerly over my shoulder, "Mr. Enoch Bone?"

Bone blinked at him as he emerged into the bright sunlight.

"Yes," he said. "It is I. And you'll be Mr. Waldo."

"Yessir, that's me, sir, Art Waldo. Welcome to Waldo World, Mr. Bone! I'm sorry about the circumstances; it's really awful that someone would want to harm the president, just awful, but it's a great pleasure meeting you, all the same!" He stopped shaking hands with Bone, maybe because he realized he was the only one doing the shaking, but that didn't slow him down. "I've admired you since I was a little boy, sir. I don't mind saying that you've been a lifelong inspiration to me."

"Thank you, I'm very touched," said Bone, guardedly, with a sidewise glance at me. "And now that you've met me, there's something you want to ask of me. Am I right?"

Waldo goggled at him, astounded.

"Amazing!" he said. "Remarkable! You probably even know what it is!"

"Do put it in your own words, Mr. Waldo," said Bone.

"You've deduced it!" cried Waldo, astounded. "You've guessed! You already know I want to do you as a cartoon character!"

Bone stared at him.

"I've dreamt of it for years, sir!" said Waldo. "Of course I would never do it without your permission. Never! Would you give it, Mr. Bone?"

Bone took a deep breath, then let it out with a smile. You never know where he'll land.

"Mr. Weston, here," he said, with a little wave, "has written down some accounts of my doings. I have read them and I think they would convert admirably into animated cartoons. Why don't you talk with him about it, once we've done with the business at hand?"

Waldo clapped his hands and turned to me and I gave him a great big grin.

"I think Mr. Bone would animate very well," I said. "My first thought is that you could draw him as a bloodhound; that way you could take full advantage of all those wrinkles. But I'll have other suggestions once I get the spare time to give the matter some more serious thought."

"I'm glad to meet you, Mr. Weston, *as* John Weston," Waldo said. "And don't feel bad about that *Folks' Magazine* business. It got the editors thinking and they've decided to do a cover story on me, after all! I hope you're up to another tour of Waldo World on our way to History Hall. This time we'll do it in the Quackycart we've specially adapted for the president!. See how the duck's neck leans back? See how the wings reach up and cover the passenger space? It's the only Quackycart in the world which is both totally enclosed and bulletproof!"

"Extremely thoughtful of you, Mr. Waldo," rumbled Bone. "I shall appreciate any concealment possible while riding in this vehicle."

Without any more help from the elves, at Bone's request, we entered the enclosed Quackycart and I saw that Debbie was once more at the wheel, but this time she was silent since Waldo himself was doing the honors as guide.

"We're following exactly the proposed presidential route," said Waldo, sitting next to Bone. "I've even instructed Debbie—she'll be driving tomorrow—to time it according to the schedule we intend the president to follow so you'll really get the feel of it. The actual start won't be much later than now in the morning, only forty-five minutes, since of course we want the unveiling of our President Parker to make the twelve o'clock noontime news. Are you ready, sir?"

Bone nodded grimly, braced himself, and the Quackycart started off with a ducky little honk since Debbie was sparing us nothing. We started off down All-American Avenue on what was essentially a rerun of what I'd already seen, but Waldo worked in some side trips with a lot of stuff that was new to me thrown in.

"This is the Haunted Graveyard, our newest ride," he said, pointing as we glided by a rugged, rocky hill covered with shaggy artificial cypress trees and a thick scattering of moldering, mossy, simulated tombs and gravestones. "After a funeral where you get buried alive, you and your family roll through it in little coffins, and there's ghosts and ghouls and dead bodies ranging from the Victorian era through the Roaring Thirties and going all the way up to a contemporary group of corpses ranging from infants to old folks, which we will keep supplied with clothes and toys representing the latest, up-to-date fads—we've only just installed a dead punk-rock group, for example—and there's a nest of giant worms, and a pack of monster graveyard rats, and at the end you get dug up by Burke and Hare, the famous body-snatchers, and believe me they're historically accurate in every detail, we're very careful about things like that. A lot of parents worry about their children seeing spooky stuff but I say nothing gives kids a better boost than a good, old-fashioned scare. Heck, I even think it helps them grow a little!"

I was happy to see us make a closer pass by the Ducky Nests than we'd made on my previous excursion since that gave me a chance to watch Bone make fists on his cane and grind his teeth at the cute, fluffy little ducklings as they frolicked with one another and winked at us, and we saw a lot of other swell stuff I'd missed before including the Lunar Village, which Waldo told us NASA might use as a trainer, and the Dinosaur Den, whose whole outside was a heap of giant bones, and the Witch's Wood, which looked like something built to punish naughty children.

Unfortunately we didn't stop at any of that, but trundled straight on to History Hall where Debbie parked our Quackycart in a special parking space directly before its entrance on the Plaza of the Past, which had just about every famous date in American history worked into its concrete so that you could push little Neddy in his stroller over the signing of the Constitution, have a minor family spat atop the sinking of the *Lusitania*, and spill your ice cream all over the invention of Fulton's steamboat.

14

History Hall was a big, spread out, domed building designed to impress and belittle the viewer, and if it gave you the funny feeling you'd seen it before, that was because it was an expert filching and shuffling together of bits and pieces of some of the most famous buildings in the world, and if you were curious, you could buy a guidebook for two dollars which would identify each and every part and impress the fourth-grade schoolteacher I think I mentioned earlier.

By the time you climbed up to its row of huge bombproof, airtight double doors by means of an outside staircase, bigger on purpose than any in Washington, D.C., you were one hundred percent awed, as you were meant to be, but that was only a softening up for your first stunned view of its interior, which did what it could to put all existing capitol buildings and cathedrals to shame by soaring as high as it could without collapsing back in on itself, and by using every swanky wall covering its designers could think of, from chunks of the Sistine Chapel to tiles from the Taj Mahal to smoky paintings of hunters on a simulated cave wall.

The place had been declared off limits to tourists for that morning, so a lot of kids would have a pretty unconvincing story when they got back to class, and footsteps echoed very impressively as Waldo walked us around, pointing out heroes and villains, people I'd never heard of before and people I'd heard of too often, and as I watched Henry the Eighth eat a chicken leg, or looked up to see Lindbergh wave from the cockpit of his plane, or was pointed at by Jesse James's six-shooter, I realized I was feeling increasingly creepy.

I hadn't been able to pin down why at first, but then it slowly dawned on me that most of these people were dead and all of them were absent. We were really alone in a great big empty hall full of gadgets built to trick us into thinking a whole lot of great folks had shown up for the party.

Probably the basic weirdness of this place is what spooked its designers and confused them into being solemn when they just meant to be serious, and that's why History Hall didn't succeed in looking like the grand, uplifting public monument it was pretending to be, but only the world's biggest and all-time most impressive funeral parlor, which is what it really was.

Of course the effect was heightened by Dr. Schauer's being there, going around straightening historical sleeves and neckties and curls like an undertaker gussying up his corpses while he smiled at all of us sympathetically. Nealy told me quietly that Schauer was definitely not going to be at the actual ceremony tomorrow since the public-relations staff had agreed firmly, down to its last member, that he was a little too creepy for public consumption, even if nobody was up to admitting it openly.

The President Parker Waldobot stood on a special platform which had been built for the reception, and it was run through the whole routine planned for tomorrow with Waldo rehearsing his part as the host and Ashman standing in for the president while Schauer sort of lurked beside them making sure that the Waldobot turned and winked at the audience, just the way Pat Parker would have done, after asking the president if it had seen him someplace before, and to be sure its expression of sincerity was completely authentic when it ended the ceremony by taking Parker's hand in its and telling him in a deep, vibrant voice: "Mr. President, I can't tell you how proud and yet humble I'll be to represent you here at Waldo World!"

That done, and leaving behind a picked team of Ashman's men to carry out a final, careful going over of the place, we all piled back into our Quackycart and were whisked to the Motel of the Future, a big, shiny pile of hundreds of terraces with rows of stainless-steel bannisters in front of silvery, one-way windows concealing rooms which you got to via exterior elevators zipping smoothly through glass tubes.

All that was pretty slick, but it wasn't the future part; the future part was that you never saw another human being, outside of the other guests, because the whole staff was automated, from the bellhop machine that rolled out and took your luggage and had a little slot in its side for tips, to the receptionist machine that checked you in after it had asked you in a kindly voice if you'd had a nice trip, all the way to the brightly colored little machines that purred in to clean your room and turn down your bed and put a foil-wrapped mint on your pillow before they wished you good night.

I expected Bone to hate the whole thing, and he did start out by saying a few unkind things about it, but when the little room-service machine brought him a pot of his favorite tea along with his favorite biscuits he made a little quip about the future being nowhere near as bad as he'd anticipated and from then on I never heard a complaint out of him.

We spent the rest of the afternoon making plans and arranging ways to carry them out, using Bone's room as our headquarters, and when Bone and Ashman and Athenee and I met with Waldo for dinner in the

Restaurant of the Future atop the Motel of the same, Bone actually chuckled at a little joke the automatic maître d' made seating us, and that led to my telling Waldo how much Bone liked the place, and that led to Waldo promising to give Bone a home-service machine which would be especially programmed for his tastes and residence.

Waldo was very interested in the Mandarin and the Professor and Spectrobert, not only because Bone figured it was more than likely we would be dealing with them the next day, but because it struck him they would make good Waldobots for a scary corner in History Hall.

"I like it," I said, and turned to Bone. "The Mandarin should be using one of those torture instruments of his with flowery names."

"Quite so," said Bone, chewing a bite of the *Omelette aux Fines-Herbes*, which is his standard fallback dish in a strange restaurant, which this one certainly was. "Perhaps something literally flowery, such as his 'Embracing Lotus Petals' head crusher, might be the answer, but perhaps that would be just a little too gory for the children. Perhaps you could have him hovering over that ghastly cage which lets rats feed on you, one section at a time, the thing he calls the 'Six Gates to Paradise.'"

"Have you made those up?" asked Waldo, looking a little pale. "Has he actually used such things?"

Bone smiled and nodded and took a little sip of mineral water.

"Repeatedly," he said. "And with considerable enjoyment. His masterpiece along those lines was a blasphemous, mechanical statue of Buddha which was able to perform a very credible variation of the 'Death of a Thousand Cuts' on its victims. The thing's a forerunner of your Waldobots actually, and when one considers how many days it takes to execute that particular torture properly by hand, one is forced to admit the device certainly was a genuine time-saver."

"I think you are making poor Mr. Waldo a little sick," said Athenee.

"Oh, no," said Waldo, waving his hand vaguely. "No, really, I'm quite interested. But I have to admit I didn't realize he was that awful a person."

"He is," I said. "But his new pals won't have any trouble keeping up with him, though they each have their little quirks. The Professor, for example, likes to make little scientific points as he kills you, if he can, such as how much of you can be surgically removed by laser beams before you're actually dead. I remember once when that kind of curiosity naturally led to his figuring out he could let a witness live and suffer for years and not tell on him, if he only removed the brain of the informant and sewed it up in the skull of a chimpanzee. We once broke in on the place he was hiding too late to save the life of the witness, but at least we were in time to prevent him from completing the operation."

"Actually," said Bone, laying down his fork and studying our host closely, "I think Mademoiselle Athenee is quite right and that we should stop telling Mr. Waldo these gruesome things. We've obviously upset him dreadfully."

"No, no," said Waldo. "Please. I'm really very interested. It's just that I had no idea these people were capable of such things. But we have to deal with them, don't we?" He swallowed. "How about Spectrobert?"

"My father," said Athenee.

"Oh!" said Waldo, startled. "I didn't know! How did he get involved with these horrible men?"

"Because he's as bad as they are," she said. "Maybe worse."

"A brutal and inventive sadist of inexhaustible appetite, our Spectrobert," said Bone. "He is, in a way, particularly chilling because no one knows his original identity, since no one has ever seen his real face and lived. He either keeps his head covered with a meticulously cut, black-silk version of an executioner's hood, or shields his features in an endless series of brilliant disguises. The essential trick of him is that he could be anybody; it lends him a highly effective sort of existential eeriness."

"He's the one I want to get," said Ashman.

Bone paused and took a thoughtful sip of water.

"He was, for instance, an exact simulacrum of Weston, here, when he very nearly killed me in a singularly bizarre mansion, bizarre even for San Francisco, atop Nob Hill. Weston himself was in full view at the time, rendered unconscious and tied in a chair, and I had ample chance to compare him and Spectrobert's imitation of him carefully. Outside of a slight variation in an arching of the left nostril, there was no discernible difference between them.

"Weston and I were in that mansion because we had been hired to protect the eccentric family which dwelt there and I am afraid we did rather a bad job of it as Spectrobert killed them all, one by one and very horribly, with the claws and working jaw of a dreadful costume he'd designed and worn for that purpose. He was, you see, posing as a family monster which the family believed they had inadvertently imported from their ancestral Scottish castle when they relocated to this country.

"It was, perhaps, the most grotesque disguise of his career; certainly effective, decidedly deadly, and I will confess that during one livid moment—when I came upon him on a darkened staircase, tearing the head of Angus McGiver off the old man's shoulders with a single twist—his skillful use of it briefly convinced me the family's hoary old superstition was, in fact, the absolute truth."

"How horrible!" gasped Waldo.

"Quite so," agreed Bone. "I still find it hard to believe that my intellect could have been so appallingly misled, but it happened, nonetheless. In any case, Spectrobert offered to remove his Weston disguise and show me his real face before he killed me with an acid-spraying device he'd specifically constructed for the purpose, but I declined out of a sense of honor as I'd observed that Weston had worked himself loose and would shortly rescue me and that, therefore, I would not die, layer by layer, according to Spectrobert's plan. To this day I'm still not sure whether my gesture was absurdly high-minded, or if I regret it or not."

"They're terrible, then," said Waldo, staring down at his plate. "All of them. They're much worse than I thought."

Later that evening, after we'd made the last plans we could think of and Bone and I were alone and I was about to leave, Bone stopped me with a little wave of his palm and asked me what I thought about Waldo.

"Just the same as you," I said. "That's why I was telling him the worst things I could think of about those bastards. Is that why you were telling him the worst things you could think of about them?"

"Yes," said Bone, sighing. "He's obviously involved."

"If we'd known about it earlier we might have turned him," I said. "As it is, I guess the best thing to do is let him run and use him as a weathervane. I don't think he'll do anything on his own, but we should always have someone right next to him, just in case."

Bone stood and walked to the window. Waldo World was still lit up, but its streets were almost empty.

"It really is a marvelous arena to meet them in," he said. He turned to me and raised an eyebrow. "Do you think we'll manage to kill them this time? Permanently? Or will they kill us?"

I smiled and shrugged, and he smiled back, and we left it at that.

Athenee was waiting on the terrace of her suite when I arrived. I joined her at the shiny railing and we put our arms around each other and looked out at the lights of Waldo World. A Quackycart with three people and an angel in it buzzed by below and the angel's glistening wings flapped in the breeze as one solitary firework blossomed in the black sky for no particular reason.

"He's almost done it," she said, "he's almost made a fairyland."

"It's easier for me to imagine the elves from up here and at night," I said.

"My father was always making fairylands," she sighed. "Of course it goes without saying they were all sinister ones. I spent my babyhood in one of them. I took my first steps in an old castle on a high, wild cliff on the coast of Brittany. All the peasants believed it was haunted by real fairies, but I never saw any, even though I searched for them.

"But then I never saw my mother, either. One night, just before I was taken off to bed, I asked my father about her and he told me she had been a fairy princess who had died of marrying a mortal, so I decided that, since I was her daughter, I must be the fairy who was haunting the castle.

"Some years later, shortly before my father was forced to leave because of a series of mishaps in his smuggling operations, a favorite kitten of mine wandered away during a beach walk and I followed after her deep into a cave which the tides had carved out of the base of the cliff beneath the castle. I found the cat curled up in the doorway of a lovely tomb set in a beautiful, salty grotto.

"The door of the tomb was made of copper and covered with a bas relief of sad, pretty angels reaching upward. Over the door, carved deeply into the coral from which the tomb was made, was written 'Athenee.'

"At first I thought the tomb had been made by my father for me against the day of my dying, but then I slowly and solemnly realized that this must certainly be the resting place of my mother's body.

"That evening during dinner I took my courage in both hands and told my father I had seen the tomb and read the name on it and he paused between one bite of *homard à l'Américaine* and the next and told me in a very quiet voice not to speak of it again. The servants waiting on the table were taken away just after dessert by rough men dressed as sailors. It was their bad luck to have overheard me.

"My last memory of the place is looking back through the windows of my father's limousine at high, chalky clouds rising like thunderheads and covering the landscape. My father had mined the castle and the cliff so that all would explode and then fold in on itself and be forever sealed off from strangers. Seeing me stare out, my father reached over and patted my hand, something he rarely did, and whispered: 'Don't worry. She is not harmed. She is safe.'"

We looked down on Waldo's try at a fairyland for just a little longer, and then we went inside and forgot it, and yesterday, and tomorrow.

15

The sun was shining and the sky was blue. Waldo World looked just like the pictures in its folder.

Bone was stationed in the command post we'd established in the private room atop Elf Castle where I'd had lunch with Waldo during my first visit, and Ashman had gone back to New York in order to travel back with the presidential party, and things were all moving along in that calm, unstoppable way they take on when you've laid your plans and all you can really do is tinker with them until the action really starts.

I was working my way to the front gate, checking out various arrangements we'd made here and there as I moved along, and chatting with agents, some in the flesh and some over a folding pocket intercom with an earplug, and it really made me feel like a member of the club.

I'd tried to get Athenee to take one of the gadgets, too, until she pointed out that if she found her father he wouldn't be at all happy to learn she was wired, but I sure did hate to see her walk off alone and disappear into the crowd without that walkie-talkie. I knew she was tough, I knew she was smart, but I also knew that might be the last time I ever saw her alive.

The press had been kept dangling until the very last moment, as per the plan. All they knew was that Parker was in New York, and all they'd been told up until an hour ago was that there would be a really dandy story and photo opportunity somewhere in the vicinity this morning, so they were all standing eagerly by because, of course, none of them wanted to take a chance on getting scooped.

Now the specifics had been given out and the media, as some damned fool has got us all calling them, came down full force on Waldo World—tv, newspapers, magazines, the whole bunch—and Frank Nealy was going crazy trying to give each reporter the impression he thought they were the most important one, and of course everybody figured he was giving the real story to someone else.

My timing was pretty good because I had just turned up at the base of the Quacky statue when everybody started making excited noises because someone with a long-range viewfinder had just spotted the presidential caravan traversing the bridge.

Nealy was there, sweating even more than usual as he checked the distance between the main gate and the steps of Elf Castle where Waldo had just made his appearance, probably imagining a couple of hundred terrible things that might prevent his boss and the nation's chief executive from meeting smoothly in Quacky's shadow.

"My mother told me there'd be days like this if I got into public relations," he told me. "I'm really going to tie one on tonight. I'm going to aim for an instant blackout."

The line of flagged limos was pulling within range of the naked eye by now, with the presidential carrier, long and gleaming, right in the middle, and I ground my teeth and wished it would turn around and leave because I didn't see any way in the world there wasn't going to be a whole lot of trouble.

I felt a touch on my arm and saw that Waldo had

come up beside me. He seemed frailer and thinner than before and the sun made him look pale and had turned the Polaroid shading in his glasses almost black.

"These awful men, Mr. Weston," he said. "I know they're criminals. I know they're very, very bad. But can you tell me, are they mad? Are they crazy people?"

"They're nutty as fruitcakes," I said, looking down at him and watching him kneading his hands. "They're a hundred percent gaga. Why do you ask?"

"Nothing," he said. "I was just wondering what to expect."

"Expect anything," I said.

The limos parked in an expensive-looking row before us and after the lesser members of the Praetorian guard had poured out of the ones before and behind, the doors of the main car opened and Ashman popped out, looking wary, followed by the president, waving and smiling, followed by none other than Hewliss; so Bone's concern must have really got through to the head honcho because under ordinary protocol he'd have left it to Ashman to handle the job.

The president turned his attention entirely on Art Waldo, who had come up to shake his hand and otherwise welcome him, and Ashman and Hewliss formed a sandwich around the two of them while the other troops acted as the wrapping. They did it just in time because now the tv people were pushing their little logo microphones in hard, and the press photographers were making that rattlesnake racket with those fancy shutters of their cameras, and of course everybody wanted close-ups.

Standing next to Parker, Waldo looked scared and cringing, almost as if he expected the president to start beating him. I saw Parker pick up on it with a puzzled expression and then reach out with his big hands and sort of pat Waldo's shoulders the way you'd soothe a nervous animal and when that seemed to be working I glanced up at the top of Elf Castle, I suppose with some idea of seeing Bone gazing down at us, but of course all that could be seen was the thick web of gargoyles which covered the whole upper area of the tower like a fuzzy clown's wig. Then I heard Bone's voice coming through the little speaker in my earplug.

"Don't worry, Weston," he said. "I see you."

"I suppose that's the important part," I said into my intercom. "How do we look? What's happening that us ants down here are missing?"

"Nothing alarming so far," said Bone, "though I confess I expect it momentarily. The band has formed and will be marching into view shortly, accompanied by a small army of people in ridiculous costumes. Outside of that and this whole grotesque place, I see nothing unusual."

"Okay," I said. "Keep in touch."

The president and Waldo climbed into the Quackycart with Ashman and Hewliss and a third agent seated behind them. The third man was especially for Waldo, and while Hewliss and Ashman mostly peered out and up and around, the third man kept his eyes strictly on the small cartoonist.

The Quackycart started with a quack from its horn, the rest of us surrounded the silly thing, and the bunch of us started off down the center of All-American Avenue with the big brass band Bone had predicted in front of us, all trimmed in gold and blaring away full blast, and a bunch of actors dressed up as cartoon characters out of Waldo's movies clowning along beside us and looking a lot jollier than the agents and I.

By now the Waldo World visitors had got the message that the president was amongst them and were pressing in for a look at their leader with their children on their shoulders, but they were a friendly bunch and Waldo's security people, all decked out in old-timey cop uniforms with big gold stars—some of them so much into the spirit of the thing that they were even wearing handlebar moustaches—weren't having much trouble managing them.

Being a policeman really puts you in the wrong frame of mind for a party. You peer past the balloons looking for lurkers and you check out the stuffed toys for suspicious bulges, and you even wonder if the little kids might be armed midgets because it's been done. You're no fun at all.

I did take in the blue sky and the sun I mentioned, and that the colors of the buildings looked as bright as I'd ever seen them, and now and then a tune the band played reminded me of long-ago Memorial Days in Elkhart, Indiana, but then I'd see something or other I couldn't make out and realize my fingers had gone under my lapel and were resting on the butt of my gun.

The worst moment before the last part came as we were passing the Haunted Graveyard, which was a little more in keeping with my mood than all this other stuff, and my heart froze and my breath stopped on the half exhale when I thought I caught a glimpse of someone dressed in black ducking behind a tomb.

"Check out the decorations on top of the graveyard," I said, talking into the pocket intercom which had somehow got into my hand, and wondering how I'd managed to push the right buttons that quickly. "Look for a big, tall guy with a black cloak and a black mask."

"You're kidding."

It was an agent named Pyle who I'd met for the first time yesterday and who thought a lot of himself.

"No, I'm not," I said. "And if it's who I hope it's not, neither is he. Get it in gear!"

I saw him and a couple of others appear from the back of the big green "D" that finished off "GRAVEYARD" and watched them spread out over the shaggy, spooky, blue-gray plastic grass and disappear amongst the fake cypress trees and tombs.

"Be careful, damn it!" I said.

The band played "The Man on the Flying Trapeze" and now and then I'd catch a quick peek of an agent bobbing out from behind a crypt or hopping over a low gravestone, but no new glimpse of the man in black.

"What's happening?" I asked.

"Nothing," said Pyle, out of breath. "There's absolutely no one here, damn it!"

"Keep looking," I said. "And grab him if you see him, and kill him if you think he's getting away!"

Then I folded up the intercom and put it back in my pocket because you might as well drop something if you can't do anything more about it, and because we had rounded the corner into Wally the Whale Way and History Hall had come into view.

We were passing by the Moon Village at a good clip when I heard my name being called and stepped over to the Quackycart because Ashman was leaning out of it looking worried.

"I heard about the graveyard," he said. "Do you think that was Spectrobert?"

"That's how he looks when he's not in some disguise," I said. "Understand, I'm not sure if it was him; it might have been a shadow, or the dark side of one of those cypress trees in a breeze. He can fool you."

"You're not an easy guy to fool," said Ashman.

"He's managed it with me in the past," I said. "I stared at him once all night long in the Louvre and never even saw him. He's one of the best. Can you persuade the president to get the hell out of here?"

"I'm trying," said Ashman. "He says only after he sees the Waldobot."

I walked along beside the Quackycart for a second or two and then I said: "I think that's where it's going to happen."

"So do I," said Ashman, then he leaned back and rolled up the window, thereby making the Quackycart once more entirely bulletproof, and I looked ahead and saw they'd cleared the great big Washingtonian staircase leading to History Hall so I trotted across the Plaza of the Past and up the steps because I wanted to have a quick look around, before the others arrived, to see if it wouldn't make me feel a little better. What happened was it made me feel a lot worse, because the agents at the doors let me through with a friendly wave since they'd gotten to know me that morning when I'd posted them, but I knew I could have been Spectrobert wearing a perfect, foolproof John Weston disguise, the way he had that time Bone had talked about last night.

The hall itself was empty of unsimulated life except for a few agents around the edges who were also dumb enough to take me at face value, and my feet made those funny echoes you get in vacant museums and large mausoleums as I walked around glaring at the Waldobots. I rounded a clump of presidents and Teddy Roosevelt startled me by suddenly demanding that I have a bully day, Lincoln depressed me as always, and I stared at Taft for being fat, but none of it got me anywhere, and anyhow we'd checked the bunch of them earlier.

I stationed myself by a piece of bunting on the side of the Pat Parker platform and watched the press rush in and take up positions in order to record the entrance of the president, then I watched the great man himself come in and take full advantage of the situation with teeth flashings and wavings of the hand and encouraging pats on the back of Waldo, who now looked so pale I wondered if he was about to faint, but he didn't; he led the way to the platform with a brave little smile. The two of them, with Hewliss unobtrusively alongside, climbed the steps side by side as a kind of gasp ran through the members of the press when they saw the Parker Waldobot stir and look pleased and then grin broadly as the two men came toward it.

"President Parker," said Waldo, in a thin, reedy voice, "it is my great honor and pleasure to present you to Waldo World's greatest technical and artistic triumph to date. May I introduce you, sir, most respectfully, to the first of an entirely new, vastly improved line of Waldobots—President Parker!"

"Glad to meet you, Mr. President!" said Parker, reaching out his hand.

"Glad to meet you, Mr. President!" said the Waldobot, right back, and the two of them shook hands as the working members of the press went totally bananas trying to get a better picture of the scene than anybody else or trying to say or write down something cleverer about it since there was no doubt this was obviously going to be the world's number-one story all the way up into the evening news unless something serious happened.

They went even nuttier when Parker and the Waldobot turned at the same moment, both with one big hand on each other's shoulder and the other big hand waving at the crowd, both with the exact same lopsided grins and the same twinkle in their eyes, and when one photographer shouted, "I've lost track!" it got a lot of giggles, and they blossomed out into laughs when someone else called out, "Which one of you is going to run for a second term?" but when both Parker and the Waldobot pointed at each other and quipped, "He is!" it started a genuine riot.

Parker and the Waldobot turned this way and that, arms about each other, both of them apparently equally skillful at giving everybody a chance for a really good picture and egging on an audience, and I looked over at Ashman and he looked over at me, and I saw Hewliss quietly move in a little closer and take a position right next to the Waldobot because none of us liked any of these goings-on at all.

Waldo stepped forward raising his arms, and in a

high quaver kept repeating, "Please listen, please listen," until it was quiet enough for him to say: "And now, in honor of our very distinguished guest, the Parker Waldobot would like to say a few well-chosen words."

The Waldobot smiled and nodded and Parker made as if to step to one side, but the thing had slipped its arm around his waist so he couldn't.

"One thing I've learned in politics," said the Waldobot, grinning, "is that actions speak louder than words."

Now Ashman was heading up the plaform stairs with me right behind him because that was nothing like what the thing had said in its rehearsal.

"Lookie here, now," said Hewliss, "just a goddam minute!" and his hands moved smoothly toward the Waldobot but not quickly enough to grab it before it had pulled a gun from inside its coat and shot him full in the face and sent him twitching back, spraying blood from the huge, horrible wound that had been his face, to flip smack into Ashman with a violent reflex spasm and push the two of them in a tangle over the edge of the platform and into the crowd below, which was now two-thirds screaming people trying to get out of there and one-third reporters and photographers working frantically on the scoop of their lives.

"They said it wouldn't *do* that!" Waldo screamed, and he grabbed the president's shoulders and was starting to tug at him as hard as he could, but that wasn't helping Parker get loose any more than the president's own kickings and pummelings, because the arm the Waldobot had snaked around the presidential waist was locked there like an iron clamp, which, of course, was just what it was.

"Stand back, please," the Waldobot said to me, I guess because I'd grabbed the arm that held the gun with both my hands. I felt a chill run through me because all there was to feel under the sleeve were cables and metal bars and somehow I'd still expected an arm, but that didn't stop me from twisting it as hard as I could with my best come-along grip, the one that reliably makes the meanest and toughest weep—not because I was hoping for pain, I knew that damned thing would never feel pain—but because maybe I could break it.

"I told you to stand back, sir," said the Waldobot, giving me an absolutely flawless President Parker smile, and it began slowly moving its arm down in spite of my very, very best efforts to keep it from happening, and all I could do was sweat and strain with all my might as I watched the barrel of the gun move lower and lower until it pointed straight at me, and then I was shot in the head.

16

The sound of someone sobbing as if his heart would break hauled me out of the darkness into a fierce headache and a kind of dazed amazement that, apparently, I was still alive. It seemed even more incredible when I squinted down and saw all the blood on my sleeves and the front of my coat, but then I remembered rule one about head wounds which was that even small ones bleed like Niagaras. Rule two was to keep your hands off them until you had some idea of the actual damage.

I must have stirred around a little during this little training review because the sobbing stopped and I heard a scuffling coming over in my direction and there was Waldo leaning over me looking like he was seeing the most beautiful thing he had ever seen in his life.

"Mr. Weston!" he cried. "You're alive!"

"Yeah," I said, working hard to sit up. "I hurt, therefore I am."

I looked around and saw the place seemed to be entirely deserted except for the Waldobots and a few figures lying on the floor, some of which looked to be Waldobots, too, and some of which didn't. Also a whole bunch of ropes were hanging from a big, round opening way up in the top of the dome which I'd never seen before. I seemed to need about five hours to take all this in but it may have been only as much as two minutes.

"What happened?" I asked. "Slowly and clearly, please."

Waldo opened his mouth to speak and then his face screwed up and he began crying again, but that didn't stop him from talking at the same time even if it did make parts of it hard to make out.

"They're crazy, like you said, Mr. Weston! They've spoiled everything forever! Everybody's dead! Everybody! And my pretty world is ruined! Just *ruined!*"

I tried to look at him carefully and that made me realize one of my eyes wasn't seeing him, so I reached up very gently in spite of rule two and touched it, and when it didn't hurt all that much I teased it open because it had only been stuck shut with blood and was working fine after all. Then I said: "Start with when I got shot. Try to go through the whole business in order with one thing after the other."

He sat down on the floor beside me and took a deep breath and then he began to recite it like a kid in school going through a lesson.

"You fell down and I thought it had killed you too, like it killed Mr. Hewliss," he said. "Then it started to point the gun at me and I remembered the switch at the back of its neck, just under the collar—I don't know why I didn't think of it before—and I turned it off and it fell down."

He pointed up at the platform and I saw an arm hanging over its edge wearing the pinstriped sleeve of the president's suit and holding the gun that had shot me.

"Mr. Ashman came up and got hold of the president, and some of Mr. Ashman's men crowded around them, and some started clearing the visitors out of the room, but they had a lot of trouble and there were fights."

He looked up at the dome for a long minute.

"It came open, up there, sort of like a flower, and those ropes tumbled out, and men started sliding down them, men with guns, and Mr. Ashman and his agents started hurrying out of the building with the president, and the men who slid down started running after them and everybody began shooting at everybody else. There was a lot of blood. I never saw so much blood."

I had grabbed hold of some of the bunting and was using it to haul myself to my feet, but I stopped sort of halfway up in an old-man pose and asked: "Did the people who slid down have a leader?"

Waldo's eyes seemed to grow wide behind those glasses and he nodded solemnly.

"Oh, yes," he said. "He was a big, tall man, all in black. It was that Mr. Spectrobert. It's the first time I've seen him in his costume. It's a cape and a mask, the one he's famous for, and he seemed to be having a fine time."

"Did Ashman get the president away?"

"They went out the door, then the others ran after them, and then I closed the side doors with the controls and locked them, and then I closed the center door by hand, and locked it," said Waldo. "I closed all the doors tight shut and then I watched them."

"Watched who?" I asked, because I was getting the definite feeling I was missing something vital to his story. I was standing now, and I tried a few tiny, baby steps away from and back to the platform, so I'd have it to grab if it turned out I couldn't walk. When it seemed as if I was ambulatory I started lurching across the room toward the center doors like Boris Karloff in one of his cheaper movies.

"You don't want to go out there, anymore, Mr. Weston," said Waldo, still sitting on the floor. "They spoiled it out there."

There weren't so many bodies on the floor as I'd expected, just two of Spectrobert's bunch and one of

Ashman's agents. The rest were Waldobots. This fracas had really been hell on the historical figures.

I made it to the two center doors and leaned against one of them in order to rest a little, and I had to stare out of the window for maybe as much as half a minute before my vision cleared of bright little dancing spots and I could begin to work on grasping what was really and truly out there, and that was quite a challenge.

It wasn't just the effects of the whack on the head the bullet from the Waldobot's gun had given me, though I'm sure that helped, it was the difficulty of taking in the enormity of what I was looking at. I would have had trouble doing it if I'd been fresh as a daisy.

"Tell me about it, Waldo," I said at last, resting my forehead on the cool glass of the window and staring out.

"There were more of the man in black's people outside," said Waldo. "They'd blended in with the crowd. They stopped Ashman from getting the president back into the Quackycart by blowing it up. They just blew it up and killed a lot of people doing it."

He stood and started coming toward me and the doors.

"People were running around," Waldo said. "All the families, all the children. Some of them tried to get in here, but I wouldn't open the doors."

Now he was next to me so we were both looking out of the windows.

"Maybe I had an idea what would happen," he said.

He turned and looked at me.

"I'm really a very selfish man, Mr. Weston," he said, and he was so close to me I could feel his breath on my cheek. "I like people to have a nice time, that's the main reason why I built Waldo World; it wasn't just to make the money. But I'm really very selfish."

"I see," I said. "So when it all started, whenever the stuff was let loose that did all this, you still didn't open the doors, is that right?"

"Yes," said Waldo, sort of dreamily. "I just stood here and watched them change into stone."

That was exactly the way I'd have put it. Their skin did look like stone, maybe some kind of gray, flaky slate; the sort of stuff they carve those angel-head gravestones out of in New England graveyards. All their flesh, including their eyes, was the same dead gray color.

Everything else about them was unaffected, and of course that made it a lot worse, that really pounded it in, because all the dead stone people were wearing their brightest vacation clothes and carrying pretty Waldo World stuffed toys and the kids were holding the strings of balloons, which were the brightest things of all. One kid, close to the door, was gripping a cone full of melted strawberry ice cream which was still a bright pink and it looked especially pink where it ran across his fat little gray stone wrist on account of the contrast in colors and values.

The body of the little kid was standing, his father was in a kind of half crouch like the statue of an ape, and his mother was just a heap of stone on the ground wrapped in a lemony dress. It seemed to affect different people in different ways, whatever it was they'd let loose on them. One man wearing a gaudy Hawaiian shirt, for instance, was pushing against the door with both hands on its handle, trying to open it the wrong way as people will do in a panic, and I wondered if I'd be able to get it open with him gripping it like that. Also I wondered if he'd be heavy or light or if he'd be solid or crumble. I found myself doing a lot of speculating.

"It was a low, gray cloud," said Waldo. "It started from over there, by the Pirate Galleon. The group led by the man in black had chased Mr. Ashman's party to the side of the ship, and then into it. I could see them fighting in the rigging like they do in the movies and the Howard Pyle illustrations. Then there was some gray smoke, just a puff of it at first, I thought a fire had broken out, but it grew and grew—it just wouldn't stop, Mr. Weston!—and when it came over the crowd it made them move slower, like a freezing river, and you could see the color leaving everyone's skin as they stopped moving."

"The air seems clear now," I said. "How long ago was this?"

"A half hour? I'm not sure. Not long."

I looked up at the sky.

"There's a bird," I said. "See him flying up there? He's not having any problems. I say it's over."

I began undoing the locks, ignoring Waldo as he scuttled back, and started pushing on the door. The man in the Hawaiian shirt turned out to be heavy, all right, but he didn't crumble, he just swung open with the door as if he'd been carved on it. I took a deep breath right away to get it done with one way or the other, and when it turned out I'd guessed right I took another.

"It's okay," I called back inside.

Waldo was back by the platform, crouched next to the pinstriped arm and holding its hand for comfort. He peered out at me, then let go of the hand and began to tiptoe to the door while I started down the steps, working my way past some of the stone people and stepping over others. Close up to them I noticed they had a funny, chalky smell which really gave me the creeps, and every so often some sight would stop me in my tracks, such as the brass band still more or less in formation with its shiny tubas and slide trombones or, worse, a little girl in a stroller with her Quacky the Duck doll in her arms, both of them staring the same stares at me with wide, blank eyes.

Waldo caught up with me by the time I was halfway across Presidential Place and asked me where I was going and I was about to tell him when my intercom started buzzing over and over in my pocket and I clawed it out as quick as I could because of a sudden rush of hope. I yanked the little extension cord out of the thing since I'd lost the earplug it connected with during the struggle with the Waldobot—maybe it got shot up—and the voice that squawked out of the speaker was like music.

"Weston? That *is* you down there, is it not? I hadn't dared hope!"

I hurt my head grinning, because, of course, it was Bone.

"Same here," I said. "I haven't used this thing because I just didn't want to know for sure you were dead!"

"You're covered with blood!"

"You've got good binoculars," I said. "I'll give you the details later, but, for now, it wasn't fatal. I'm heading for the Pirate Galleon with Waldo, if he tags along, because I understand that's where Ashman and Spectrobert and the president ended up. Any news?"

"Merely more confusion," said Bone. "No sign of the Mandarin, but that flying violet splotch is on the prowl, so be careful. I'm entirely alone up here. The agents ran out of the place, every man jack of them, hell-bent on avenging the death of their leader and the recapture of their president."

"I'll leave this gadget open on your channel," I said. "Call out if you see anything interesting."

Now and then amongst the stone people we came across a rare flesh-and-blood dead body from either Ashman's or Spectrobert's armies, shot and killed before the gas spewed out. They started getting more numerous as we approached the galleon, and there was a regular heap of them when we got into the shadow of its hull.

Outside of our breathing there wasn't a sound except for the occasional flap of a sail or a kind of soft whisper the wind made going through the rigging. I carefully wiped my hands on my jacket since they'd suddenly become a little sweaty, got a firmer grip on my gun, and we were halfway up the gangplank when I froze because, mixed in with the wind sounds, I heard someone softly calling my name, but saying it *Jean*.

The ship's railing was a long row of seagoing Spanish nightmares carved in wood and painted in gold, and she was looking down at me from between a scaly dragon and a merman with a trident.

"There's no one else," she said. "No one alive."

I hurried up the gangplank and she hurried to me, and we held each other close, just to make sure we were both really there.

"I thought you were dead, too," she said, after a while.

"They kept missing the vital parts," I said. "How about you? How did you ever manage to keep alive in this place?"

"I saw my father rushing through the crowd with his men and called his name," she said. "He swerved over to me, killing two people with his broadsword doing it, swept me up, and the fighting brought us here."

Still holding her, I looked around.

"A pirate galleon's meant for slaughter, at that," I said. "It looks just right covered with bodies and blood."

"It sounds mad, but I really believe the place inspired them all," said Athenee, "both sides. It was an incredible battle. My father and his men won it—they were, after all, the pick of the world's assassins—but the others fought marvelously well. Mr. Ashman alone must have taken half a dozen with him at the end. You'll miss finding him if you don't look up."

Ashman was slumped in the rigging, but he had a foot each on two others tangled in it beneath him, and still had a hammerlock on the dead man who'd stuck the final knife in his chest. It's how it would have looked if Errol Flynn had lost to Basil Rathbone.

"Good for you, George," I said. "You died a hero."

"I never knew his Christian name," said Athenee.

"We never used them with one another after our first meeting," I said. "I suppose it's because we were a couple of tough guys."

"He was a nice man," said Athenee. "I liked him. I'm glad he died not knowing he'd been fooled."

"What do you mean?" I asked.

"Come over here," she said.

She led me around a huge mast and there, sprawled half upside-down over an open chest filled with phony jewels, was the body of President Pat Parker.

"Damn," I said. "We blew it."

"Don't be so hard on yourself," said Athenee. "Watch this."

She grabbed a capstan to brace herself and kicked Parker hard in the side of his gut, which made him immediately sit up, smile broadly and say, just a little too quickly and too high in tone, "It's a real honor to meet you folks!" before he fell back with a thump and a rattle.

"My father figured out how to do that," she said. "It took him a dozen kicks to do it, and he enjoyed each one of them better than the last."

"It's a Waldobot!" I said. "Ashman got himself killed saving this goddam machine!"

"And my father went to a great deal of trouble kidnapping it," said Athenee. "He thought he was double-crossing those other two by stealing the president for himself, but they were too clever for him and used his own double cross to double-cross him. I can tell you, John, it made him madder than I ever saw him before, and I have seen him mad quite a few times, I can assure you."

I stared at her.

"So that's why he used the gas," I said.

"That's why the gas," she said. "He gave me a mask

and put on another, none for anyone else, and then he opened the canisters. He'd planned to do it anyhow when he'd escaped, since he told me he always hated this place, its jolliness mainly, I suppose, but now he did it just to kill his partners."

"Where is he?" I asked her. "I suppose he got away again?"

She looked at me.

"No," she said. "He didn't leave, not this time. He's over there, waiting for you, on the other side of the ship."

He was standing by the golden railing, leaning on it with his black gloves, looking out at Manhattan across the Hudson. My gun was suddenly in both my hands, pointing at the black silk covering the back of his skull, but Athenee touched my shoulder and quietly pointed out the streak of stone-gray skin showing between his mask and the collar of his cape.

"He was looking out at the city," she said, "telling me what he planned to do with it, when I plucked away his gas mask. He turned, and there was a moment when he could have killed me, but then he looked back across the river exactly as you see him."

I came closer to him. I had been this close to him only twice before, once when he almost killed me.

"I never saw his face," I said.

"I may be the only surviving person who has," said Athenee. "I was seven, I think. I came across him in his study. He was absorbed in the floor plan of a building. I could have looked at him longer, I suppose, but the sight of him set me screaming and he noticed me."

I reached up and placed my hand gently on the back of his mask.

"He always respected you, John," she said. "He hated you, of course, but he always respected you."

I let my fingers rest on the smoothness of the black silk just a little longer, then lifted them slowly from it and let my hand fall empty to my side.

"It's more than you'd have done for me, you old bastard," I said, standing back. "But what the hell, I'm a nicer guy than you were, so it figures."

Then the intercom started buzzing and I hauled it out.

"Yes?" I asked.

The little speaker clicked and Bone's voice said, "I've just seen that absurd Waldo creature scuttle off the ship, but now I've lost sight of him. He's probably ducked into one of his blasted secret tunnels."

"Damn!" I said. "I'll give you the details later, but the wrap-up is that he switched presidents on us during the ceremony. Anthenee's with me and she's alive, she's all right, but Ashman and all his men are dead and I'll fill you in on the details later. Spectrobert is dead, too, really and truly, and I'll fill you in on that, too, but I was sure you'd want to know. For now, we'll head back to the hall and see what we can do."

"No," said Bone. "Leave the ship as quickly as you can, but stay on the dock, preferably in a cleared area."

We'd just stepped off the gangplank when I heard the chopping of a helicopter growing steadily louder and looked up to see a scrunched-up version of Quacky the Duck flying toward us in the clear blue sky.

"You are looking at the world's only Quackycopter," said Bone, over the intercom, "and I am in it. As you see, we are heading for a landing by your side. Enter the instant we land and, with luck, your boarding may go unobserved."

I turned to Athenee, who was staring up wide-eyed at the smooth descent of the Quackycopter's fat white bottom.

"As you work with him through the years," I said, "you'll come to learn he's always full of surprises."

17

I hauled a sliding door open, we clambered in, and I hadn't finished slamming the thing shut before we were sloping off into the air so fast it wasn't two seconds before the Pirate Galleon looked like a pretty golden toy.

"The miracle of flight," I said, gazing down at it. "You wouldn't believe how horrible that thing looks close up."

"I've no doubt," said Bone, who was squatting behind the pilot's seat, holding the barrel of an automatic rifle on the neck of our old friend Debbie, who was doing the flying, since apparently she could work wonders with anything that looked like a duck. "Please follow my example and sprawl upon the floor so that you are not easily visible through the windows. The purple splotch is extremely active."

"Hi, Debbie," I said, squatting down, and she shot me a quick, mean look, like the sharp-toothed Foxine did in *Goldilocks*. Bone waited until we'd got settled and then began to speak.

"I suppose it would be best to start by explaining our present situation," he said. "I did not allow myself to be entirely idle after the agency's men dashed off to bare their steel, but involved myself in a variety of activities, including a careful examination of the aerie atop Elf Castle. Needless to say I found yet another secret panel, this one reached by manipulating unicorn horns and wizards' staffs carved into the paneling, and discovered a second hidden elevator whose buttons gave one the interesting option of rising one story higher."

"There was another hideaway above the dining room?" I asked.

"Of course I could not resist looking into the matter," said Bone, refusing to be hurried, "so, after arming myself with this formidable rifle from the agency's stock, I took the elevator up and found myself in a well-equipped hangar, cleverly hidden from the eyes of the curious by a festoon of gargoyles, containing this Quackycopter."

I squinted as a bright, quick flash of purple light poured in from the windows.

"Be sure you keep yourselves low," said Bone. "It's watching this thing carefully, though I think it missed your embarkation. If you can't see it, I don't think it can see you." He cleared his throat and continued. "In any case, I had barely taken in the implications of the helicopter when the elevator doors closed and I heard it descend. I climbed into this machine at once and when Miss Debbie, here, took her present place I put this gun by her jugular, where you now see it, and this quite naturally led into a longish talk which has resulted in our present arrangement."

"Which is?" I asked.

"Because I have promised not to kill her, she has given me some very useful information and will deposit us at a rear entrance to History Hall to which she's handed me the key." He reached into a pocket and waved a rectangle of silvery plastic. "Once the key has opened the door she will be free to leave, though I have strongly advised her, for her own safety, to wait outside for whoever emerges triumphant from the struggle which will surely follow."

He slipped the plastic back into his pocket and ducked slightly at another bright flash of purple.

"As to that," he said, "while we were observing the presidential parade from atop Elf Castle, the purple splotch spent considerable time appearing and disappearing outside the windows—teasing the agents, I suspect; it seemed to lose interest in the place once they'd charged off to battle—but not before I had the opportunity to take a number of revealing instant snaps."

He fumbled in another pocket, spread some photos of the purple whatsis out on the floor of the Quackycopter, and waited for us to examine them. I saw he'd made little circles on their centers around what first seemed only to be a kind of smudgy, pale blur.

"What's this fuzzy business?" I asked. "The thing's canopy? Some kind of rocket flare coming from its side?"

"Dismiss all such mechanical images from your mind," said Bone, resting his finger on the largest pale area of the blur, "and imagine that to be an enormous forehead. An ominously familiar forehead."

I studied it for a moment.

"And those two dark blurs beneath as deep-set eyes," I said.

"Exactly," said Bone.

"It's the Professor," said Athenee. "Painted by Seurat."

"You have him." Bone nodded approvingly. "That is not a vehicle at all, but a kind of window in space, and the Professor is looking out at us from inside of it. Do you recall, Weston, those extraordinarily interesting notations we came across in his little hideaway under the Thames?"

"All that stuff on the blackboard in his study?"

"Precisely. I transcribed them, at some risk, before the river flooded the place, and when I had an opportunity to study them again at a more leisurely moment, I realized they were nothing less than profound speculations bearing on the possibility of projecting three-dimensional matter through a five-dimensional continuum. The material has created quite a stir whenever I've presented it to experts, and I suspect the Professor is now in a position to make some very interesting additions to those original formulae."

The floor of the Quackycopter slanted and I saw the dome of History Hall spreading out beneath us. We went down like a rock, then landed like a feather in the side street where Waldo had led me through the gloomy garden; only this time Bone, after pressing the handle of the rifle into my hands without taking it off Debbie's neck for a second, headed straight for the rear of the Hall, then turned and waved us on after he'd opened a small door in its high, white wall.

Athenee hopped out and I followed, looking back every other step as I ran just in case Debbie had a gun hidden somewhere, but I'd barely made it to the door before the Quackycopter's blades spun faster and it began to lift.

"Immediate flight," murmured Bone, shaking his head. "Her very worst option."

He'd barely got that out before the purple splotch popped into view and sent out a nasty, spinning, yellow beam which began by making the Quackycopter glisten as though it was covered with spangles, and finished by turning it into something shrunken and black which was too light to fall in one chunk, but drifted apart in curly bits and pieces.

"Now we know why they never found a trace of that fighter plane," I said, but nobody was listening because both Bone and Athenee were smarter than I was and had already gone inside.

The tunnel was even simpler and tougher than the ones Waldo had taken me through on the way to

Schauer's workshop. The walls were nothing but stain-
less steel, as was the ceiling, with a thin line of fluorescent light running the length of its center, and the floors
were something black and hard which gave good traction.

There was a brand-new element in the decor, though,
in the form of gray stone bodies frozen in various
positions: some of them standing at their posts, some
flat on the ground with their weapons or other equipment spilled out in front of them. So either this place
wasn't as climate-controlled as the Hall of Presidents,
or, more likely, somebody had been dumb enough to
open a door at just the wrong time in order to see what
was happening, and had found out.

We made our way down a long straight hallway,
ducking around or stepping over bodies, until we
reached a stainless-steel door with another of those
brass handprints. We'd barely stopped to study it before
the three dead, gray-skinned guards standing by it
indicated they were not dead at all by aiming their
weapons at our heads, and the door slid up and open to
reveal the tall, bent figure of our old acquaintance, the
Professor, who smiled and gave an amused little shrug.

"It's so easy to ignore cadavers," he said, "especially
when there is such a plentitude of them!"

He watched the gray guards take away our weapons,
then made a little nodding bow, waved his long, pale
fingers at the room behind him, and stepped back into it
to let us enter.

"Won't you come in?" he asked, watching us carefully
as we did it, his head swaying from one of us to the
other, his eyes glinting like shiny black glass in their
deep sockets.

The room took up the same hospital-green coloration
as Dr. Schauer's place, and was laid out in the same
efficient way, with lots of tidy shelves and neatly labeled

panels. A high green curtain faced by a line of chairs cut off the view of the rest of the room after about ten yards.

"Rather different from your usual cozy," said Bone, looking critically around him. He pointed at the curtain. "I suppose your dimensional toy is hidden behind that?"

The Professor started slightly, then he raised the mats of spiderwebbing he used for eyebrows and gave a wicked old grin.

"Of course you would have anticipated it," he said, chuckling, then he frowned. "I've long suspected the London calculations were not erased in spite of my clear orders!" He reached out with his pale, bony fingers to grab a handful of air, crushed it, and muttered: "I was right to let the fool drown." Then he grinned again, waved at one of the gray guards, and the curtain started to open. "Do be my guest, Mr. Bone. You are admittedly not a bona fide member of the scientific community proper, but I can think of no one more capable of appreciating the diverse possibilities of this device. Pray do examine my toy, as you style it."

It was an open half dome, laid out like a hybrid between an airline cockpit and the control cabin of a spaceship. A large, high-backed seat faced the open O of a circular panel whose walls were crowded with a mass of complicated instruments. Behind this central chair, obviously the pilot's seat, a curved row of four smaller chairs was mounted to a raised black arc of flooring which formed the gadget's outer edge.

"The dark, circular aperture the controls are ranged around functions both as a viewing port and, when reached by those steps, as an exit," said the Professor, walking over to his machine with his hands clasped behind his ancient, black Prince Albert coat.

"Have you exited it as yet?"

"Not so far," said the Professor, "though I have used

it, as you have seen, to project my carbonizing ray with great effect."

He paused and took hold of his lapels with a gesture he'd probably developed years ago when he stood before his students.

"So far, Mr. Bone, I have traveled only as an observer, but, oh, the things I've seen!"

He paused, looked up, and rubbed his hands.

"The Himalayas, for instance, the very tops of 'em. And I've seen the bottom of Mindanao Deep, as this window takes enormous inward pressure. And outward pressure too, for—oh, Bone, you'll envy me this!—I have seen Mars!" He pointed triumphantly at his face and croaked it out, loud as he could: *"With these eyes, I have seen Mars!"*

He paced a step back and forth to calm himself, and then went on.

"But I've surpassed even those experiences. I've achieved the illuminations which mystics have striven for in vain throughout the centuries! I have cleft the rock and observed that which has heretofore burned unseen!"

He glared wildly at us in a half squat with his fists in the air like an excited old gray monkey about to start hopping around in its cage at the zoo; then, maybe because it had dawned on him that he was tiptoeing on the edge of a fit, he lowered his hands carefully, blinked, pursed his lips and moved his face around until it got back something of its professorial calm.

"A technical point you will find interesting, Mr. Bone," he said. "While transiting hyperspace I have found it is just as many theorists proclaimed it would be: One finds oneself to be entirely reversed, both left to right and inside out. It is a thoroughly remarkable and disturbing sensation, but flesh and blood is not at all the same on the other side of our three-dimensional Möbius strip as it is on this, so that while total reversal is undeniably quite awful when first experienced, one finds one grows accustomed to it and shortly one learns to function in that bizarre and surreal condition. Happily my final calculations have conclusively assured me that the reversal will occur again, returning me to this, my normal condition, when I reenter three-dimensional space at some other point."

"Let us sincerely hope for your sake that is what does occur, Professor," said Bone, with an ominous edge to his voice, "as I imagine being inside out would put even a person as resourceful as yourself in a thoroughly awkard position."

The Professor stared at Bone for a moment, then gave him a really dangerous frown, and nodded coldly.

"Quite so," he said. "Well, in a moment of inspiration, I imagine I can make some adjustments which might produce exactly that effect on certain passengers. Yourself for instance. Perhaps, when we have finished with our present business I might find the time to carry out just such an amusing little experiment, now that you've suggested it."

"It iss zo nice to zee old friends make the jokes mitt one another," burbled a voice from one side, and we turned to see Dr. Schauer glide into the room, pushing before him a rolling gurney with a sheeted body strapped on its top, just like Frankenstein, with Waldo cowering along behind him as the mad assistant in order to complete the picture.

The body on the gurney was doing a pretty good job of writhing in spite of all the straps, and when it finally managed to heave its head clear enough of the sheet to rear it up on its neck and look around at the room, there was the face of President Parker, all right, but from the way its eyes were bulging and from the look of terror it was wearing, I was pretty sure it had to be Parker himself, since nobody would ever have programmed an expression like that into a Waldobot because it would have frightened the kiddies.

His head jarred to a stop when it pointed toward us and he cried out: "Mr. Bone, these people are crazy! These people are out of their minds! You've got to do something about them at once!"

"I shall do what I can, Mr. President," said Bone, calmly.

Dr. Schauer patted Parker gently on the shoulder, then smiled up with a lot of yellowed teeth showing.

"I am pleased you have managed to be present at our little moment of triumph, Mr. Bone," he said in a harsh, hissing voice that made the small hairs on my neck quiver.

Bone looked him up and down.

"I'm so glad you've dropped the accent," said Bone. "I found it to be one of your most tiresome."

Schauer said nothing in reply to that, only reached up and took hold of the back of his head with both hands in order to slowly and carefully peel off his hair and face.

"My God, what's he doing?" cried Parker, pulling away from the sight of Schauer's horribly collapsing features as far as his straps would let him. "My God, he's a Chinese gentleman!"

18

"**M**y robe," hissed the Mandarin, spreading his arms, and a stone-colored guard gently slipped a blood-red sleeve over the long, curving nails of each extended claw. "My cap," he breathed, and carefully, held reverently with both slate-gray hands, a black cap with a bright ball of coral fixed to its top was settled on his high, bulging skull.

He sighed, comfortable to be himself again, and shook his bony body gently into place. Then he let his green cat's-eyes travel over each of us in turn.

"I see there is no need for introductions," he said, "since we have already met. Mr. Enoch Bone and myself, in particular, have met."

"As you say," said Bone. "In particular."

"How many times has one of us been absolutely sure he had at last destroyed the other, Mr. Bone?" asked the Mandarin. "How many times has one of us seemed to see the other's body burned or crushed or torn beyond repair? How many times have I raged to learn you've once again survived?"

"Far too often, I am sure, my dear Mandarin," said Bone. "It has definitely been a frustrating business for us both. Perhaps, this time, we can finally settle things between us. As an example that such relationships can be effectively terminated, permit me to inform you that

Spectrobert is dead. 'Really and truly,' as Mr. Weston put it."

The Mandarin's eyes widened, then he clenched his fists in front of him and bared his teeth in what seemed to start out as a snarl, but developed into a spreading grin.

"Excellent!" he barked.

"I was afraid you'd be pleased," said Bone.

"Do be disappointed, Mr. Bone: You are indeed a bearer of good tidings!" hissed the Mandarin. "That childish, operatic creature killed all my men but these three with his statue gas. Did he die in pain? Did he suffer?"

"Mr. Weston has the details," said Bone, but when the Mandarin turned his glittering green eyes in my direction I had to shake my head and smile in sympathy.

"He died peacefully," I said, "with his daughter by his side. Making plans to destroy New York City."

"It's true," said Athenee. "He was imagining the aluminum eagles on the top of the Chrysler Building melting down its sides."

"You too," said the Mandarin, meaningfully, after a pause. "Both of you. I remember you, Miss Athenee, as a very rude little girl. You teased my marmoset, do you remember? I have not forgotten!"

He finished that last off with a kind of bark, then dismissed us by turning to a gray guard by his side and waving a talon at the president.

"Unstrap this public fool," he said, then turned to Waldo. "You free his legs. The two of you, get him to his feet."

Waldo hurried to the foot of the gurney to obey, but when he'd unbuckled the band running over the presidential ankles he stopped and stared up at the Mandarin with a worried frown.

"Didn't you hear what they were talking about," he asked, "as we came in?"

"Of course I did," said the Mandarin.

"Well, then," said Waldo, "aren't you afraid we'll all be killed? They were talking about that machine! How it might turn us inside out!"

Bone tsked, which is something he only does when he wants to annoy, and the Mandarin knew it.

"Dear me," said Bone, indicating the Professor's machine with a sidewards wave, "you don't mean to tell me there is actually some plan afoot to travel in that thing untested?"

The Mandarin looked at Bone scornfully.

"You disappoint me, Bone," he said, then plucked Waldo forward by his sleeve. "This one is a bottomless pit of fear and trembling; there is no end to his pathetic trepidations. But such cowardly talk from you is quite unexpected."

"Before we get to all that," said Bone, "I should like to ask you something out of simple curiosity: How did you manage to make that man your creature? Particularly, how did you involve him in a plot against the leader of his country, since, in reading numerous puerile articles on Mr. Waldo in preparation for my visit to his ghastly fairground, everything I've come across indicates he is an eminently patriotic fellow and devoted to President Parker in particular. I would have thought a traitorous act of this nature would have been, for him, almost psychologically impossible."

"You have described the precise reason why I used him as my tool," said the Mandarin, pulling the cringing Waldo even closer to him. "I knew the president would never believe this miserable entity could plot against him, that he would therefore walk trustingly into any trap involving him. And it worked, Bone. All your many warnings were quite useless, were they not?

"This man had gone blind," continued the Mandarin, speaking softly, almost gently, and, putting one claw on the top of Waldo's head, he began kneading it with his nails like a cat kneads a pillow. "He kept it from the public because his advisors had told him it would bother the children. But he could not see his Waldo World, he could not draw his duck."

Suddenly, with two swift moves, he plucked off Waldo's glasses and pinned his arms to his sides.

"Look, and see the gift that only I could have given him!" the Mandarin cried with a triumphant squawk, pushing Waldo forward, turning him this way and that to compensate as he writhed and twisted, trying unsuccessfully to hide his face from us.

"That is very sad," said Athenee.

At first glance it looked as if some lunatic had stitched the frame and lens of a goggle into each one of Waldo's eye sockets, and done it crudely to boot, since the skin that was sewn to the tiny holes bored into the frames' edges seemed to be bunched and stretched more than was necessary, but as the Mandarin mercilessly shoved Waldo's head closer to us, I saw the steel irises roll, I saw the glass pupils dilate and contract. From the way they pinched the red, swollen flesh as they moved, it was obvious they caused him pain, but the things were working eyes.

"You see the horror in their faces?" the Mandarin cackled, bending his head down, hissing into Waldo's ear. "You see how disgusted they are at the sight of you?"

"Hardly at him, Mandarin," sneered Bone, "rather at the one who has done this thing to him. My congratulations; it is quite an accomplishment. No one but you could have produced such a sublime medical achievement and then degraded it so completely."

"But wait," the Mandarin snarled at us, "you have not yet seen it all!" and I was surprised to realize that in spite of all the years I'd dealt with the crazy bastard, I'd never understood how mad he really was.

"You have them in your pockets." He turned, his tall

body arching over Waldo's, and shouted at him like an angry father. "I know you always have them. Give them to me!"

Then Waldo tried even harder to break away, but the Mandarin did something particularly vicious which made him howl in agony and scrabble out two round, white things from some hidden place in his coat.

"*Look* at them," the Mandarin hissed, holding them out in front of us, rolling them around in his palm so we could see the blueness of the irises. "Precisely like his original flesh. See how they even quiver? I was going to fit them into his skull when we had finished, I was going to render him that supreme kindness, *but no more!*"

He spread his fingers, turned his hand until the eyes rolled off and dropped to the floor, bouncing just a little, and he was actually beginning to lift his foot when Bone roared at him like an old lion.

"*Pull yourself together, sir!*" he thundered. "If you want me to have any respect for you at all, you'll leave off this ghastly play. That poor wretch has done his best to do your devil's work. You have the president because of him. Return him those baubles. And try to do it with some dignity!"

The Mandarin, his leg still raised as in a T'ai Chi posture, studied Bone carefully for a moment, then let his foot gracefully return to the floor, beside, not on, the eyes, as Waldo fell to his knees and gathered them up.

"They are not baubles," the Mandarin said calmly, "they are miracles."

"As you will," said Bone.

"This has been a ridiculous demonstration," said the Professor. "Thoroughly ridiculous."

I wasn't taught in his kind of school, but I bet headmasters there stand the way he was when they're thinking of how they'd really like to cane some student.

"Ah," said Bone, "we had forgotten your faulty machine."

"I have told you that my calculations leave no doubt as to the safety of an exit at some other point," the Professor said, with his chin up and trembling like an angry turkey's.

"Are you seriously proposing that the lives of your associates," said Bone, "not to mention this extremely valuable hostage, be risked in a completely untested device? By the way, Mandarin, what exactly do you intend doing with the president?"

"We shall hold him hostage, as you say," said the Mandarin. "For a fortune. The crime will have the shock of innovation, and the Americans will pay dearly for him. Then we shall return him, but he will be altered."

He turned to the president, now standing beside him with a gray guard holding his arm, and tapped him on the top of his head. "Here, just under his pompadour. I will, of course, see to it that the scar is undetectable. He will be totally receptive, thenceforth, to all suggestions from myself."

He paused, stood back, and stroked his cheek thoughtfully with one long talon, examining the machine.

"I dislike admitting it, but Bone's point is well taken, Professor," he said. "If you are mistaken not only will my plan be compromised, the world could lose me before I have fulfilled my historical mission and that would be an intolerable tragedy. The device must be tested."

"This shows a most offensive lack of faith in my abilities," said the Professor, drawing himself up and bringing his swaying head to a rock-solid stop.

"Merely prudence," said the Mandarin, making a tiny little bow.

He walked to a console near the machine, flipped a few switches, and a huge gray area glimmered on the far wall.

"Observe a television camera mounted on the ceiling

of the Professor's machine, directed to look through the porthole." He pointed to the glimmering. "On that screen is what it sees. In this fashion we have journeyed indirectly on previous excursions with our learned friend, observing by proxy the wonders he has seen. We placed another camera to show us the craft's interior, but the images it sent from hyperspace were totally chaotic, so we abandoned it. I think that last item is a particularly clear indication there may be some risk in exiting from the machine at another destination."

"I have proven the total lack of danger scientifically. There is no disputing my figures," the Professor said, snapping it out. "You have my word on it."

"Pshaw," snorted Bone, turning to the Mandarin. "You know the man's a megalomaniac, unable to tolerate contradiction. Assurances from such a person are useless."

The Mandarin's green eyes shone and dimmed.

"We must see a test," he said, with a tone of total finality.

The Professor shrugged because he saw it was hopeless. As he walked to his machine, I felt a nudge from Bone's elbow, and started watching him out of the corner of my eye.

Bone had his hands clasped in front of him in order to pretend he wasn't doing anything with them, but, making tiny moves, he tapped himself with his forefinger then wiggled it at the guard on his right, and when that produced a look of understanding in my eyes, he transferred the point to me then wiggled in the direction of the guard on my left. After that he raised and lowered his eyebrows and I did the same back to him and we both turned to watch the Professor's demonstration.

It looked even fancier turned on, with something like two hundred dials and oscillators all lit up and pretty, and the round port in its center had started to throb and glow in a shade of violet I'd come to know well. The glimmering screen on the wall brightened and pretty soon it was giving us a repeat image of that part of the laboratory we could see for ourselves in front of the machine, so the tv monitor was working fine.

"It is functioning properly, of course," said the Professor, then he turned in his chair and looked back at us, framed in the violet disk of the porthole which was now shining steadily and brightly, his fringe of hair glowing like a halo.

"I won't forget this, Bone," said the Professor. "Mark that."

Then he turned back to his controls, pulled down a lever at either side, and he and his machine both were gone.

"Observe the television image," said the Mandarin, indicating the screen with one robed arm. "The angles are difficult to follow, are they not? The shapes are difficult to read. One's eye cannot trace the outline of any image without experiencing sudden, inexplicable reversals. There is a definite sensation of nausea. You are seeing hyperspace from the port of the Professor's machine."

"Marvelous," said Bone. "Magnificent. The man's a genius, no doubt of it. What a pity!"

The Mandarin shot him a green glance.

"Because he did not choose your righteous path, Mr. Bone?" he sneered, his teeth glistening in the bright, violet light from the screen.

Bone looked at him and may have been about to reply, but then the tv screen seemed to go black and it was a moment before we realized our eyes were only adjusting to a night scene: a stretch of empty road edged with boulders with rugged mountains beyond them, and a flat, moonlit sea for a background.

"The Professor's machine is now on the other coast of

your country," said the Mandarin, smiling smugly. "Safely beyond any pursuing officialdom."

He paused and leaned forward, and so did we all, because we had seen the frame of the porthole swing open. Bone nudged me again, and I edged just a little closer to the guard he had wiggled at earlier.

Then something glistened at the bottom of the screen and something else, bent and dripping, waved across it, and then the Professor flopped out into full view in the moonlight of the lonely West Coast road.

I think, then, all of us, with the possible exception of the Mandarin, screamed.

"The blunderer," snarled the Mandarin, "the fool! He has killed himself! He could have killed me! *He could have killed me!*"

"But he's *not* dead!" shrieked Waldo, watching the thing up there extend a groping part of it ahead to leave a slimy red trail on a boulder. "Look, look, you can see his heart beating on his outside! You can see his lungs puff up and empty! Filling! He's still alive! Oh, God— he's *still not dead!*"

I went for the guard at my side then, because he had forgotten all about me, and I grabbed his gun away from him easily, because he had forgotten all about that too, and Bone did the same with his guard, his guard's gun, and we killed them both, just like that, and Bone shot the third guard and I shot the Mandarin, but he was dodging through a door beside him which hadn't been there before and all I managed to do was blow his left arm into bits just before the door closed, and then I remembered that didn't count for much because the arm was only metal and plastic since I'd shot his flesh-and-blood arm off years before, so I guess that shows you I'm getting old.

19

"**D**on't be too hard on yourself, Weston," said Bone, ducking his head as he passed beneath a bat-winged demon carved on the underside of a low stone arch, "you had no way of knowing he was standing by an exit."

"He's always standing by an exit," I said, holding a hand in front of my candle because walking this fast made it flicker and I didn't want it going out.

"I wish he wasn't alive," said Waldo, who was the leader in our trip through this weird place because it was his tunnel and he was the only one who was familiar with all its strange little tricks. "I know he'll try to kill us! That's how his mind works!"

"Surely," said President Parker, giving us a dumb smile all around as we hurried along, "he won't hurt us *now*, will he? I mean, all he'll be doing is fleeing for his life!"

Bone sighed.

"Mr. President," he said, thumping his cane just a little louder then necessary, "up to now, I have not invoked any of the privileges of age, but you must understand that all of this has been extremely wearing to me. Here I am, for example, hobbling at top speed, carrying a candle that is dripping burning wax on my hand, because, years ago, it was decreed company policy at Waldo World that tiny, flickering flames should be the only means of illumination provided in this bizarre underground tunnel which Mr. Waldo has seen fit to decorate as a sort of ancient catacomb, complete with sepulchers piled full of automated skulls which gnash their teeth and rattle their jaws as you walk by."

"Some of the skulls have rats in them which are automated, too!" said Waldo, and Bone glanced at him.

"I am sure some of them do, Mr. Waldo," he said. "Exactly my point. To continue, Mr. President, if I am to survive the last phase of this business and be of some assistance to you, I really feel I must insist that you abandon this compulsive optimism, as I find it particularly wearing. I know it will be very difficult for you, that it will go against the very fiber of your being, but please do indulge me."

"Of course, Mr. Bone," said the president, looking a little puzzled. "I'll be happy to do anything I can."

"Excellent," said Bone, brushing a dangling plastic spider from his face, and then he turned to Waldo. "You say you were entirely unfamiliar with the door the Mandarin used?"

"I never saw it in my life," said Waldo. "And none of our secret panels do what that one did—weld themselves shut. It just doesn't make any financial sense to build a doorway you can only use once."

"So he's loose in some tunnel whose route and connections are entirely unknown to you," said Bone, "and you've said you're only vaguely familiar with many other alterations and projects he's involved himself with during his association with you these last two years or so."

"I let him do what he wanted to, Mr. Bone," said Waldo, looking at him with those steel eyes of his showing because no one had bothered to hunt up his dark glasses in the mess we'd left behind. "I know it was wrong of me, but that's what I did."

"So what do you think he's up to?" I asked Bone, swerving to avoid the clutch of a bony plastic hand.

"Exactly what Mr. Waldo said he was up to," he muttered. "One way or another, he's setting out to murder us. Indiscriminately. All of us."

"But surely he won't want to kill the president, Mr. Bone!" Waldo gasped.

"Why not, sir?" Bone asked. "He has no further use for him. The Professor's machine was to transport his captive safely away, but it's proven a ghastly farce, and Spectrobert's gas has killed off all his soldiers and thereby eliminated the possibility of any extempore alternative. No, Mr. Waldo, the only pleasure left him is our destruction, and since you tell us that this catacomb leads directly to the base of that monstrous duck statue, which is to say to a point a mere few paces from the front gates of this establishment, the chances are he'll try to kill us here, in this macabre place."

"Something ought to be done about people like that," Parker said peevishly, maybe trying to show he wasn't optimistic.

"Quite right, sir," said Bone, glancing at him. "Hopefully, we shall."

"Are you thinking about the sort of things the Mandarin plays with?" I asked Bone. "Trapdoors? Or spikes from the walls? How about guillotines from the ceiling? All these stalactites would hide them pretty neatly."

"Good heavens!" said the president, lifting his candle up for a closer look.

"I haven't ruled it out," said Bone. "But it seems unlikely since this tunnel was originally constructed as an ordinary passageway for the Waldo World staff. I suspect the attempt, or attempts, will be of an invasive nature. Knowing the Mandarin, I imagine he will do his best, even in executing an impromptu attack such as this, to use means as esthetically appropriate as he can muster."

"You mean whatever he uses," said Athenee, "it'll have the right feel for an underground cemetery."

"Precisely," said Bone.

"I don't know," said the president, sighing. "I just don't know."

We went on a little further in silence after that, and were passing an extended series of open niches containing skeletons in rags which softly rattled as they writhed, when Waldo suddenly held up his hand and we stopped in a bunch with our candles flickering.

"What is it?" said Bone. "Do you see something?"

"No," he said. "These eyes aren't that good in a dark place. I smell something. Something musky. It's true what they say, you know: The other senses compensate."

"I got it, now," I said, after a few sniffs. "Animals. A lot of them."

We peered ahead and then, as if we'd rehearsed it like a dance team, all of us wheeled at once and peered behind. Sure enough, a few bright red eyes just missed dodging out of sight quick enough to fool us.

"They sneaked back up around a bend in the tunnel," said the president. "Mr. Bone, what are those things?"

"I am very sorry to have to tell you that they are wolves, sir," said Bone, after a grim pause. "Special pets of the Mandarin which I've encountered before, but never in this disadvantageous a situation."

"Not your ordinary wolves, mind," I said, holding my candle a little higher, and wishing it was a lot brighter. "The Mandarin wouldn't bother killing people with ordinary wolves."

"They are gigantic survivors from the Pleistocene epoch," said Bone. "They should have died out with the mastodons, but one of the Mandarin's agents, a professional Transylvanian hunter, came across a pack of them in the Carpathians. They are huge, quite terrifying creatures and it's highly possible that sightings of them and slaughters by them through the ages have contributed to some of the dark legends of that area."

"They're perfect for an underground cemetery," I said to Athenee, and then I looked over the gun I'd taken from the gray guard and made a little announcement to the group at large. "I hate to tell you this, but I don't think I have that many bullets."

"And I have no idea what's left in the clip of the weapon I've purloined," said Bone.

"Nor I of this one I took," said Athenee. "And these three guns are all we have. That doesn't seem much to offer a pack of Pleistocene wolves. Am I pronouncing that right?"

"Yes," I said, and to Bone: "Maybe we should make as much distance as we can while those things are still in the skulking mood."

"No," said Bone. "They've let us have a glimpse of them and that means they've started toying with us. If we try to go on they'll start by plucking one or two of us off from the rear. Once we'd fallen into the inevitable panicky scramble, they'd fall upon us and feast. We'll have to do something clever. Now."

Bone peered into the darkness thoughtfully, then bent to study a skeleton scrabbling pathetically at the heavy, half-closed lid of its stone sarcophagus.

"These things move," he said to Waldo. "How much more can they move?"

"They can do pretty much what I want them to," he answered. "They were the prototypes of the Waldobots, actually. It was easier and cheaper making them skeletons instead of people during the experimental phase. Fun, too."

"How do you animate these bones?" asked Bone.

"We've got hidden controls scattered through the tunnel," he said. "Let me show you."

He walked over to a pale stone coffin with a sleeping knight in full armor carved in marble on its lid, and when he pulled at the handle of the knight's broadsword, the panels on the coffin slid this way and that, a keyboard floated into view, and the thing turned into a kind of Gothic organ.

"We call it a Xylobone," said Waldo, smiling, putting his fingers on the keys. "It's funny, you know, I would have told the Mandarin about these, but he never thought to ask."

He played a couple of notes and a skeleton sat up in its niche. He played a few more and it swung its legs over the niche's edge and slid to a standing position on the floor.

"Pretty neat, huh?" asked Waldo, and I said: "Pretty neat!"

"Make it walk," said Bone. "Make it walk until it stands under the center of the tunnel's arch."

Waldo played a few more notes and the skeleton obediently tottered to the center of the tunnel.

"Now make it reach up," said Bone, and when Waldo had doodled a couple of high notes the skeleton did; but the tiny bones at its fingertips missed the peak of the ceiling's curve by a half yard.

"Blast," said Bone. "But bring out some more of them, bring out a lot more. Form a line of 'em from one wall to the next. And hurry, I've seen those wolves' eyes flicker into sight three times now as we've done this."

Waldo played a spooky little fugue upon his Xylobone and, one by one, and then in little, shuffling, rattling groups, the skeletons crept out from dark, cobwebby holes in the walls; clattered out of rusty, hanging cages; sneaked from sewers whose lids they'd pushed aside. Bone watched all of this carefully and issued another command when the first rank of them were standing in a wavering row.

"Have them clutch each other," he said, "and have

the outer ones clutch the walls. Make that one there grab hold of that chain; make the one on the other end embrace that stone angel."

They formed a double row, and then a third, each time locking themselves together according to Bone's instructions, building a thicker and thicker wall of plastic bones.

But on the other side of that wall the wolves were growing braver. They started by making quick darts out and back, first only one at a time, then in twos, then in swirling little packs. After that, one bold wolf came out and sat and stared at us.

"My God," said Athenee, "that's not a wolf; that's a bear!"

"In its day, mademoiselle," said Bone, "bears were the size of elephants, and elephants grew hair. That thing had to compete with saber-toothed tigers for its prey. You will note its frontal fangs are typical of the era, being as big as the blades of Bowie knives, and curved to hook the victim into its bite. I imagine a man's entire forearm could fit comfortably in its mouth."

He turned to Waldo and said: "Have the skeletons form a fourth rank, and I think there are enough now to support some of them climbing up on top to extend the wall to the ceiling. Always have them embracing; entangle them as much as possible. I must say the effect is quite Hieronymus Bosch."

Now there were four huge wolves squatting in the open; their red, dripping tongues hung and swayed from a foot and a half to two feet from their mouths as they panted and drooled and watched the skeletons moving, and watched us behind the skeletons. Suddenly, so quickly that he'd done it before you'd realized he'd started, the nearest and the largest of them had sprung up, darted forward, wrenched one of the skeletons loose from the wall. He dragged it to a corner where he tore it into chunks, and then he threw the chunks across the floor in all directions, furious because he'd found they held no meat.

The other wolves prowled and sniffed the plastic rubbish. One or two of them actually broke a few bones open and bent the steep rods inside with their teeth, and when they realized their proper prey was not the skeletons at all but the people hiding behind them they squatted again, but this time in a much larger group, and stared through the bones at us with their red eyes, making wolfish plans.

Bone had orchestrated six ranks of woven skeletons into the wall by now, and was working on the fourth rank in the group of the top, which was plugging the gap to the ceiling, when that same boss wolf which had led the pack before suddenly lifted into the air and hit that top row hard enough to make the whole wall bend back and totter. But it held.

"More of them, Mr. Waldo," said Bone: "More of them as quickly as you can."

Waldo bent lower over his Xylobone's keyboard and played it even faster, but he looked at Bone over his shoulder and shouted: "We're just about out of them!"

The huge wolf had not slipped back from the top of the wall, he was still up there and, worse, he was fighting his way through at its very top, where Bone's weaving of skeletons was thinnest.

"Everybody get your guns pointed and ready," I said. "I don't know how much it'll take to stop that thing, but I'll bet it turns out to be quite a lot!"

Bone, Athenee, and I formed a triangle and aimed the barrels of the weapons we'd taken from the gray guards at the center of the top row of skeletons. We watched it bulge more and more under the pressure from behind and then saw it erupt outward in a shower of plastic bones as a gray paw as big as my head with claws spreading out in front of it like a fan of ivory knives burst through, followed immediately by a huge hairy snout snarling around a set of teeth that would send chills down your spine if you saw them in a glass case on a dusty skull in a museum during a rainy afternoon, but which definitely froze your blood when viewed under the present circumstances.

Bone was closest and in the center and he didn't hesitate to put what was left of his ammunition, I'd say about ten rounds, right into the center of that snout, but it keep coming, with eyes on top of it which were glowing like coals, all of it framed by a huge headful of iron-gray hair with each strand bristled out straight as a nail so the whole thing looked like a hairy explosion.

Athenee and I kept our fingers on the triggers since we'd long ago lost all interest in placing single shots, but now there was a second paw, and now there were huge red ears like those that sprout out from the sides of devils' masks at Halloween, and both our guns were only clicking when the bulk of its shoulders heaved into view, big as a bear's shoulders just like Athenee had said, and I was wishing I'd thought to save a bullet for her because of what was likely to happen next, when the shoulders sagged, and the snout gave a final gnash and went still, and the paws spread just one more time each and folded and the goddam thing was dead.

"Let's get out of here," snapped Bone, because the wolf was twitching and jerking again, not on its own this time, but because the other wolves were tearing at it from behind. "They'll eat their way through him in no time, if we linger, and be on us!"

We hurried down the rest of the tunnel as fast as Bone could hobble, and Waldo was just pulling open a big iron door at the end of it when we heard a crash and a howling in the dark behind us, and after we'd all scuttled through the door and out, and just before Waldo and I finished pushing it shut, I saw the first wolf padding round the nearest bend full tilt, and then Waldo pushed a huge, black bolt that looked to be exactly what you would ask for to seal things off in a catacomb, and when that bolt had slid solidly into its sockets I didn't mind the thumps and clawings and growls and yelps on the other side of that thick, solid iron door at all. As a matter of fact, they were almost a kind of music.

20

"**S**o that's it, then," said President Parker as Waldo opened the outer door with its view of the entrance to Waldo World only thirty or so yards ahead. "We're free!"

Then he turned with a grin.

"I hope you won't accuse me of undue optimism this time, Mr. Bone!" he said.

"It is difficult to err with too much caution when dealing with the Mandarin, Mr. President," said Bone. "He is still alive; therefore he is still quite dangerous. Make no mistake, that is an active battleground out there. Observe the casualties."

And he waved a hand at a gray stone family group which had been gaping up admiringly at the statue of Quacky the Duck towering above them when the gas hit them, and still were, and would forever, unless someone took pity and carted them away.

"By the way," I said, "the casualties have company. Waldo wandered out there when no one was looking. I think he's brooding."

Bone and I moved to the door and looked out and there was Waldo, standing in the sun, gloomily studying the little stone family.

"He is obviously depressed but he doesn't appear to have seen anything particularly alarming," said Bone.

189

"Ah, well, someone had to play the advance scout, and I suppose it might as well have been our Mr. Waldo."

"How is everything out there?" I called out to him, and he turned, sagging and sad, and gazed back in at us.

"They killed all these people, Mr. Weston," he said.

The yellow Quacky balloon the little stone girl standing next to him was holding blew into Waldo's face. He let it bounce against his cheek a couple of times and then he brushed it away.

"Is it quiet out there?" I called out. "Does anything look fishy? Do you think it's safe?"

He looked at me, shuffled around in a slow circle, staring outward, then shrugged and nodded.

"It looks perfectly safe, Mr. Weston," he said. "I don't see anything danger—"

But he stopped talking to me, right in the middle of the word *dangerous*, because something orange and flat and big as a house had suddenly come crashing down.

I rushed to the door to see what sort of amazing new event had happened, but the thing's impact had stirred up a brown cloud of dust as thick as fog, and all I could make out in the swirling dirt and rubbish was a kind of huge orange column which, even as I looked, moved up, and another kick of dust puffed out and stung my eyes as the first enormous thing sailed up after it, and by the time the air had cleared enough for us to get any kind of a view, there seemed to be nothing visible except the bare ground.

"This place is extraordinary," said Bone. "Nothing less than extraordinary. What in the world was that? Where in the world is Mr. Waldo?"

"I don't know, to both," I said. "But I guess I better find out before it happens to the rest of us."

I ducked out sidewise and flattened myself against the golden side of the pedestal that supported the statue of Quacky, and stared about me every which way, but, just like Waldo, I couldn't see anything dangerous, though I was smart enough not to admit it out loud, being a professional.

Very, very cautiously, I detached myself from the wall and took a couple of steps outward, looking carefully around me, but still I saw no sign of anything unexpected. Nothing lurked on the pedestal beside the Quacky statue, no one appeared to be sneaking from one group of stone corpses to the other, nothing strange was flying in the sky.

I prowled over the ground where I'd last seen Waldo standing, with the idea I'd find him right away as a great, big bloody splash, and when that didn't work out I started looking for subtler traces, and when that didn't pay off either, I had to settle for becoming increasingly confused.

I could see Bone peering out of the doorway, watching me go through all of this, and it was obvious he was experiencing a little confusion of his own.

"Is there no sign of Waldo at all?" he called out.

"Not a speck of him," I called back.

The little stone family was there, all right, but crushed level to the ground, the girl's red balloon included. I stood staring down at the flatness of that balloon, wondering about mortality and so on and getting nowhere with it, when I suddenly realized I wasn't standing in the sun anymore, I was standing in dark shadow, and I knew I hadn't moved.

I put two and two together and may have broken all private detective broad-jump records, but we'll never know because the ground joggled, every part of it in my vicinity, and the dust cloud came again, and so I carelessly rolled away from the post where I'd landed without stopping to mark it.

I continued to roll until I was clear of the cloud and then got up and ran until I was far enough away to get a look at the whole thing from a suitable distance, then I stopped and studied the vista.

Once you got some persepctive on it you saw the cloud was big, but not all that big, since it only covered the area around the gold pedestal, and only rose up to the bottom edge of Quacky the Duck's checkered coat.

I stood at a half crouch, all ready to run some more if I spotted anything coming out of the cloud after me, but when it slowly faded it was still the same old view as before and just as bare of clues.

Then somebody did about as good a job of making me jump out of my skin as was ever done in the course of my entire life by the simple act of clearing his throat directly behind me. I spun around, clawing by reflex action for the gun I no longer had, and there, hunkered down next to the aproned stone body of a hot-dog salesperson, was Waldo.

"What's doing this, Mr. Weston?" he asked.

"I was hoping you could tell me, Waldo," I said, "and it's something of a disappointment to learn you can't."

Then I heard someone shouting my name repeatedly and turned to see Bone poking his head out of the pedestal's door, peering around with pretty obvious concern, and I'll have to admit it really flattered me to see how relieved he looked when he saw me standing there waving at him.

"Weston!" he shouted. "I thought that thing had got you!"

"I'm fine," I said, "and so is Waldo. But neither of us has any idea of what's going on."

"Confound it," said Bone, after a pause, "I've had enough of this!"

He started coming out with Athenee and the president. I saw he had his jaw set and my heart sank a little because he gets a little unreasonable when his jaw sets. We damn near lost San Francisco one time when he got his jaw set.

"I'm not sure if you should come out from under there," I said. "My honest opinion is that it's probably a pretty bad idea."

"There are wolves behind us," said Bone, stomping full ahead with his cane now, talking as he stomped. "There are ossified cadavers all round us, and now some infernal device we seem totally unable to understand appears to be skillfully zeroing in on this absurd hiding place of ours, threatening to crush it and us to powder at any given moment. I am not saying there are not risks, there are always risks, but I think the time has come for us to take them and leave!"

He and the others were further out now, and still coming and I still didn't like it. I was about to say something calm and reasonable and hopefully persuasive along those lines when I realized Bone and the others were now walking in a shadow, a kind of fan-shaped shadow, and then I looked above and saw the huge, orange, fan-shaped thing that was casting that shadow. It was Quacky the Duck's foot, and it was raised, and it was ready to stomp.

"It's the duck!" I yelled at them. "It's Quacky! It's the goddam duck! Run! It's coming from above!"

A long time before I'd finished all of that, and a good thing for them, Bone and the others had started going as fast as they could, and it turned out to be only just fast enough because when that big orange foot hit the ground its lead toe was a bare yard away from Bone's behind.

Once more a huge cloud of dust spread up and out in all directions, hiding everything from view, and I heard Bone gasping and clumping in my direction way before I actually saw him and the president come flailing into sight with all their upper parts dusted with a fine, sprinkling, like powdered-sugar doughnuts. The president brought his dash to a halt by my side, but Bone's idea of a reasonable distance was apparently about two yards farther out because it was only then that he stopped and turned and threw a wild-eyed glance back at the duck.

"Astounding," he wheezed, whirling the tip of his cane upward to point at the duck's head. "You'll observe there's actually a kind of control room built into that stupid thing's hat. See the window that's opened just over the brim? And there's the Mandarin himself, the villain! I can see him there crouched over some levers!"

By now the dust cloud had almost entirely settled and I didn't like what I saw, or rather what I didn't see.

"Where's Athenee?" I asked.

Bone glanced around.

"I don't know," he said. "I thought she was by our side."

I started to head back toward the pedestal but Bone lunged forward and grabbed hold of my arm.

"Let go of me," I said, because I didn't want to be rude and just pull away, but he tightened his grip instead and leaned closer to me.

"She's extremely competent, Weston," he said. "I understand your concern, believe me I do, but there is every reason to assume she has taken good care of herself. Run back there in a knightish effort to save her and that ridiculous thing will only flatten you. I assure you your Athenee would not appreciate the favor."

He was absolutely right so I relaxed and he let go and I cupped my hands around my mouth and shouted "Athenee! Athenee!" as loud as I could, but there wasn't any answer.

"Only someone totally devoid of any sense of humor could possibly put himself in such a position," growled Bone, glaring up at the Mandarin who was looking down smugly at us from inside the duck, which now stood with one foot on and one foot off its pedestal. "I'm absolutely certain he believes we are observing him with solemn awe and has no idea how ridiculous he has made himself look by placing himself inside that feathered pile driver!"

The duck's shoulders gave a funny little shrug at that point and its other foot stepped off the pedestal and landed with an earthshaking thump alongside the one already on the ground. All through this operation the head was turning so that the observation window in its silly cap, and the steady green gaze of the Mandarin inside, kept pointing straight at us. Now the duck was shorter by a pedestal, but somehow it suddenly looked a whole lot bigger.

"It's unattached," said Bone, in a completely different tone of voice. "It's loose. It's mobile. This may be serious."

"For heaven's sake," said President Parker, pointing. "Look at that, will you? When that thing moved, its coat swayed forward and I believe I caught sight of someone over there, on its side. Yes! See? Look there! Do you see over there? Toward the duck's rear? Climbing up the side of its coat? Just coming over the top edge of the flap on its left pocket?"

With every question he jabbed his finger in the duck's direction again until Bone hissed: "Make him stop that damnable pointing! That thing's wings are stirring. If the Mandarin sees her he'll brush her off like a fly!"

"Oh, ah, yes," said the president. "I hadn't thought of that!"

"No offense, sir," I said gently but firmly, and, taking hold of the presidential arm, I lowered it as unobstrusively as possible.

"It's Athenee," whispered Bone. "Employing her second-story burglary skills, by gad. Admirable!"

The wings bent at the elbows and swung around a little in their checkered sleeves and I thought for a second maybe she'd been spotted, but then the duck leaned over and reached out to put a huge, three-fingered hand on either side of a handy tower growing out of Elf Castle and worked the thing back and forth a few times with a terrific noise of timbers snapping and guy wires twanging, and then ripped the whole business out by its roots.

The duck straightened, made a half turn, swung the tower back and forth a few times like a Highland thrower getting the feel of his javelin, then heaved it in a smooth, arching toss so that it landed with a terrific crash lengthwise across the opening of the entrance.

"Couldn't be neater," I said. "He's plugged us in. Do you suppose he sneaked out at night and practiced with that thing?"

The duck's head swung smoothly back in our direction as it took its first step forward, crushing a row of welcome booths along with their bright little flags, and when we saw how much closer to us that one step of his towering orange leg had taken him we wasted no time in working our way back to the fence.

The Mandarin sat up there in the top of his duck and watched us do it, and only when we'd reached the fence and the end of all possible retreat did the big machine take its second step, which was all it needed to tower directly over us with the toes of its big orange feet only yards away.

"What is all this?" the president asked in a small voice. "I don't understand. Are we doomed?"

"It may be so," said Bone gloomily. He turned to me. "Realistic humility and simple good sense always forbade my dismissing the possibility of our eventual destruction at the hands of one or another of these villians, Weston, but I must confess that never—no, not even in my most disconsolate speculations—did I ever visualize a defeat this outrageously pathetic!"

I glanced down at him glaring at the Mandarin.

"All the same," I said, "I still think he looks silly in that duck."

Bone looked at me, then back at the Mandarin.

"You're right," he said, grinning. "He does. He looks a perfect ass."

Then I jumped, because President Parker had suddenly grabbed my arm, like a kid does when he's excited, and was whispering loudly in my ear.

"Look up there, Mr. Weston," he said. "I don't want to attract his attention, I don't want to point, but *look up there!*"

I did, and then, without moving my lips, without moving anything I absolutely didn't have to, I spoke to Bone in a low, steady voice out of the corner of my mouth.

"Up there," I said. "Working her way up to the front of the thing's jacket."

"I see her," Bone said. "Going up button by button. Absolutely extraordinary. By heavens, Weston, I've never seen such sangfroid in my life, indeed I have not!"

"What if he looks down?" hissed the president.

Then as if on cue, the huge head of the duck did start to tilt and we could see the Mandarin in his aerie in the little green hat peering carefully this way and that over Quacky's big, broad, orange bill.

"What am I going to do, Bone?" I asked. "How am I going to save her?"

At that instant, with a smooth swing upward, Athenee crouched neatly under the giant red carnation fixed to the front of Quacky's checkered coat.

"You needn't bother playing the hero, Weston," Bone chuckled. "She's saved herself."

"We've got to do something," I said. "He'll see her sure if we don't!"

Suddenly, without any warning, Waldo shot forward, heading for the wide gap between the duck's legs, then swerved when the right one shifted quickly. When they slammed together the moment before he would have made it through, he skittered around and started heading back.

"She's taking advantage of the distraction," whispered Bone, "she's heading up. There's a proper woman, that one! Oh, it's a good thing for my career as a consulting detective that I never came across any such as her in my younger days!"

Waldo scrambled back over the top of the duck's right foot and headed south along the fence as the Mandarin flicked his talon over the levers and made the big machine swing smoothly around to follow him.

"Look at her moving low across that thing's shoulder," murmured Bone. "I'd have married her, by gad, that's what I'd have done, and for certain!" He paused, mildly astonished. "And I'd have enjoyed it, too! Yes, I really would have, and that's a fact!"

The duck slammed a foot down in front of Waldo, not to kill him, only to cut him off. It was obvious the Mandarin was becoming interested in the torture. Athenee had worked her way around to the back of the duck's neck, come across a large white panel, and opened it. She was reaching in now, and tugging firmly and with great interest at some stuff inside.

"And if she'd turned me down," continued Bone, "I hope I should have been silly enough to waste the rest of my life in mooning over my loss, for I would have enjoyed that, too!"

The duck stomped playfully to the right and left of Waldo, who was now scrambling around in a total panic, but the second stomp had a little less authority to it, and that had to be Athenee's doing because she'd come across a great big glob of electronic spaghetti inside the panel and was enthusiastically pulling out yard after yard of brightly coded wires braided together like Rapunzel's hair. Sparks poured from the wires as they tumbled out and little arcs of bright blue light danced between them.

"She's got him!" cried Bone. "Bless her heart, the darling—*she's got him proper!*"

The duck turned, leaving Waldo forgotten and free to crawl to safety, gave us a few comic nods and a great view of the Mandarin determinedly trying to track down the glitch, then lurched unevenly away from us and started stumbling down along the fence, executing an occasional pointless hop or salute. Athenee began swinging down the back of the duck's coat, going easily from one handful of checkered cloth to the next. The colored wires were throwing out showers of sparks now, and patches of the coat were starting to blacken and flame.

Suddenly the duck wheeled around, giving us a clear view of the Mandarin in a total panic, frantically clawing at the controls like a long, lean jumping jack, and Bone laughed aloud.

"Look at him! He's in a total tizzy, the rogue, in a blind spin! This is simply delightful, Weston! I wouldn't have missed it for the world!"

The Mandarin clawed out and grabbed a lever, obviously at random, and it turned out to be a magnificently bad choice because the duck froze and stared into space as though something brilliant had suddenly occurred to it, then it grinned that ridiculous grin children all over the world love because it means Quacky is about to do something hilarious, then it looked straight in our direction and opened its beak wider than you would have dreamed it could.

"L-U-C!" it blared at us, full volume, far louder than it had done when standing on its pedestal, welcoming all those families, all those kids, "LOOKIE AND SEE!"

"He blundered onto the dingus that starts off the 'Lucky Duck' song!" I said.

"How extraordinarily droll," murmured Bone. "How absolutely perfect. He must be furious! He must be raving!"

I saw Athenee swinging gracefully from the duck's tail like the greatest trapeze artist ever, and then, with a smile and a wave, she dropped out of sight.

"She's thrown you a kiss, Weston!" cried Bone, clapping me on the shoulder. "You mustn't let that girl go, old chap. You really mustn't, you know!"

Now the duck began jumping clumsily from side to side in a kind of mad jig, heaving the Mandarin helplessly back and forth inside its little green hat.

"K-Y-D!" the duck sang, this time even louder, even more enthusiastically, and the Mandarin, in a last frantic try at control, was flailing at every button and lever within reach, but it only made things worse, and all attempts at correction only made things worse yet, and in the end the duck took off seemingly totally on its own on a crazy, zigzag waddling.

"YESSIR, BY GEE!" the duck howled gleefully and, impossibly, even louder, as the Mandarin hauled at yet another wrong lever which sent Quacky stumbling off away from us in the direction of the high cliffs overlooking the river.

"That's done him!" said Bone with a totally satisfied chortle. "That's finally finished him off!"

"I'M QUACKY!" bellowed the duck, easily kicking its huge feet through the high fence that walled off the rest of the world and shuffling across the highway with its stalled cars and their stone passengers, "I'M QUACKY, THE LUCKY DUCK!"

Then it stuck an enormous wide-spread webbed orange foot into empty space, tumbled with a grin over the edge of the high palisade, bounced from one rocky collision to the next, and finally landed with a loud, echoing belly flop onto the Hudson with its bill deep into the water. So if it was doing any more singing, it was only for the fishes.

Epilogue

Waldo survived, as did his new eyes, so we'll have a chance to see if they work as well as the Mandarin claimed they would. He'll go to trial of course, but we've all testified, the president included, that his brave wild run at the end probably saved our necks, and that should help.

Bone thought about it and decided not to look at whatever Spectrobert's face was, either, in spite of years of curiosity, and the French government had him buried in the cemetery of Père-Lachaise in a very French gesture which I kind of liked, but nobody went along with my suggestion of using him for the monument.

The Professor's body created a lot of confusion amongst the California Highway Patrol, but after a few explanations from us, his body was autopsied and his clothing and ID were found neatly sealed inside his outside.

Nobody in officialdom was all that bothered when they didn't find a trace of the Mandarin's body. They pointed out that the duck's head had been split wide open by its tumble over the cliffs, and patiently explained to us how that gave the strong river currents a chance to sweep the corpse away, but Bone and I both wish we could have seen him dead.

The president was really pleased at not being kidnapped and turned into a zombie, so he asked Bone if he wanted any favors and first Bone said he didn't, and then he thought it over and said that so long as the government had ruined my retirement, the least it could do was to set up another of my choice, and I said that would be fine, but they'd have to include Athenee in any plans for me.

They did, and it's all very secret, but because this is just between you and me, and since we're friends, I figure I can go so far as to tell you that the south of France sure beats the hell out of Elmsville.